WAKEFIELD PRESS

MARS IN SCORPIO

Kurt von Trojan's partly autobiographical play *Mars in Scorpio* won the prestigious Pater Award and an Ian Reed Radio Drama Award and was produced and broadcast by the ABC. His *The Transing Syndrome* was acclaimed as "the best science fiction novel to be published originally in this country" (Bruce Gillespie, *Thyme*). He has successfully self-published another fantasy-satire, *Bedmates*, about the alienation of the individual in an AIDS-stricken society. "It's gripping stuff . . . often mordantly funny and full of sharp observations about where our present society is going" (Katherine England, *The Advertiser*).

His early experiences made him aware of the power of indoctrination and the authoritarian state and his novels and stories examine the place of the individual in mass society. As a journalist, he wrote extensively on environmental questions, his articles appearing in newspapers as far-flung as *The Washington Post* and *China Mail*.

T0357927

Mars in Scorpio

Kurt von Trojan

**Wakefield
Press**

First published 1990
Wakefield Press
43 Wakefield Street
Kent Town
South Australia 5067

Cover image by Andrew Stock and Stephen Bowers

Made and printed in Australia.

Design and layout by Tabloid Pty. Ltd.,
97 Sturt Street, Adelaide 5000.

Typeset in Goudy by Adelaide Phototype Bureau Pty. Ltd.,
163 Halifax Street, Adelaide 5000.

Printed by Hyde Park Press Pty. Ltd., 4 Deacon Avenue,
Richmond 5033.

ISBN 1 86254 257 0

To Margaret Peters,
never forgotten

BY THE SAME AUTHOR
The Transing Syndrome
Bedmates

With thanks to Michael Bollen who put himself on
the line and helped make this a better book, to my
editors Jane Arms and Peter Day, and to Beverly Allen-
Sympson and Jody Nancarrow for their encouragement
and support.

Promotion of this title has been assisted by the South
Australian Government through the Department
for the Arts.

1

cologne, west germany, oct 15, reuter - otto kaiser, 'the mongol' of sachsenhausen concentration camp, went on trial here today for the murder of more than 10,000 prisoners during world war two.

kaiser, 51, and nine other camp staff, allegedly drowned prisoners in sewage, beat them to death, or hosed water down their throats until their bellies burst.

they are also said to have used a method known as 'squirting a-la sachsenhausen'. prisoners were lined up in the cold, squirted with a hose and left to freeze.

THE SHEET of teleprinter paper is yellowing. I strike a match. The head rasps against the side of the box and hisses into flame which, yellow rimmed with blue, catches the paper and eats into the page. It flares up, curls, blackens, shrivels, and the print disappears; the ash collapses. I strike another match. More paper – notes, clippings, letters, photographs – one blazing sheet lights the next. I feed page after page into the fire, blinking at the heat. Glowing specks float and dance in the air, biting smoke fills the kitchen, and a black mass fills the sink.

I burn my past. Twenty years of reporting, writing.

I burn The Book.

Sweat runs into my eyes. A speck of soot has lodged under my right eyelid. I rub the eye with the back of a salty hand, and lurch to the bathroom. My face stares back at me from the mirror. I pull down the stretched pink eyelid over the red-veined eyeball. I see a dark head of tangled hair, the forehead lined, a bristly beard greying. I blink, and the eye waters: the tears wash out the speck of soot.

Smoke drifts through the house, and I cough and throw open the window. There is a blast of heat from outside. The hills are parched yellow. In the valley a jackpump clunks and shrieks.

I pick up the telephone, slippery between my sweaty fingers, and spin the dial. Engaged. I try again. Engaged: she can talk for hours. Disgusted, I bang down the receiver.

When did we last make love? Was it last month? Last year? She sat on her couch, the gold velvet one with the gold velvet cushions, and I knelt at her feet, my chin on her knees, and looked up at her upturned nose, raven hair, and eyes so dark that her pupils and irises melt together. My finger traced her lips. Could she read my thoughts, my sadness at the transience of things? She grows roses in her garden. A few days earlier they were in full bloom, but now the petals have fallen.

I lifted her blue and white striped summer skirt and buried my head in her lap. Under her skirt it was safe. Her skin was cool, and she smelled of perfumed talcum powder. She uses deodorants, shaves her armpits and her legs. I wish she wouldn't.

We went to bed. Afterwards we lay and talked. There haven't been many women with whom I have enjoyed lying afterwards. But now her husband is back in town, Jack, the Big Wheel, the Media Executive, the Man with Power.

I snatch up the phone and I dial once more. This time her phone rings. I wait, impatiently. She can't have gone out. Please let her answer; I must hear her voice. Her phone rings and rings until I'm disconnected.

I must have missed her by seconds. I wonder if she would have assured me of her love if she had answered, assured me that I was still the Only One, that nothing had changed between us. Or would she have clicked off after a whispered, 'Jack is here. I can't talk now?' Or after a brusque, 'Ring me some other time. I'm terribly busy'? Has she gone away without telling me? With Jack? Or is there someone else? The Reverend Christian Cleaver? Jealousy consumes me.

Why do I torture myself? Why do I persist with this nonsense?

I stumble about the house naked. My skin is on fire, and I can't bear the touch of clothing. I can't see because I'm not wearing my glasses, which hurt the bridge of my nose. The jackpump clunks and shrieks. All my frustration, my pent-up rage, focuses on the mindless piece of machinery. I'll destroy it, short-circuit the motor, jam the flywheel, tear the wretched object bodily out of the ground with my bare hands.

Squinting, I fumble with the record player. The pickup arm slips, the diamond skates across the record. Haydn's 'Emperor' is ruined. I resist the impulse to hurl record and turn-table across the room and flick on the tape deck. The voice of Adolf Hitler, rough, guttural, rhythmic, hammering, rasps from the speakers in a torrent of aggression greater than my own: 'A small clique of criminal elements who are now being exterminated without mercy!' I rewind the tape and play it again: 'A small clique of criminal elements who are now being exterminated without mercy!' Rewind. Play it again. I can't remember how often I have played that tape over the years. It is wearing out. Ghosts of the past.

The eyes of Adolf Hitler stared at me from my schoolbooks and from the classroom wall: bright blue, luminous, hypnotic. The Fuehrer watched over us like a father. He fought untiringly for our victory, never took a single day's holiday. But on his birthday he invited the children to strawberries and cream. We all wanted to be invited by the Fuehrer to strawberries and cream.

A small clique of criminal elements who are now being exterminated without mercy!

I sat on the fringed red and blue rug and to this day, the pattern is etched on my memory. Traitors had tried to kill the Fuehrer. My mother stood by the black, square box of the radio listening to the Fuehrer tell the world that he was alive. There was a strange expression on my mother's face, and she was white, her eyes glittered. I was too young to understand it all, but my mother's face told me that something very important was happening.

The bombs came.

And then they took down the pictures. They cut pages from our schoolbooks or pasted them over. What they had taught us until yesterday was today monstrous and wrong.

I learned the names 'Auschwitz' and 'Belsen'. Soon, I was no longer a German. I was a Jewish refugee on the way to Australia.

I burnt my papers: notes, clippings, letters. The Book. The photographs of Ingrid. I must put the past behind me. Ingrid walked out and slammed the door on our twenty years of marriage.

Cynthia is not here when I need her.

The newspaper is limp in my damp hands. *Miscellaneous: Social and Matrimonial.* People looking for people. I must find someone else. I look down the column. The gays (AIDS-safe group forming), the married men (daytime meetings, discretion assured), the predators (generous businessman for fun times), the swingers (couple, seeks similar). The single mothers. The middle-aged divorcees.

My finger halts.

ATTRACTIVE, intelligent, unconventional, freethinking woman,
40s, wishes to meet non-plastic
man. Reply ʙ213 Advertiser.

Unconventional and freethinking? In bed? I find pen and
paper. I suck the pen and chew my beard. Dear ʙ213? Dear
attractive, intelligent, unconventional, freethinking woman. I
think the same . . . What about the 'non-plastic' bit? A plastic
formulation. Warning bells ring. What have I got to lose? Has
she got AIDS? Sooner or later we'll all catch it. Dear attractive,
intelligent, unconventional, freethinking woman. Would you
care to contact a writer, guaranteed non-plastic, recently
divorced . . .

With a thrill of anticipation, I run my tongue over the
back of a postage stamp. Now I will have to go out into the hot
sun to post the letter before the box is cleared. It will give me a
chance to buy food. I haven't eaten for two days.

2

THERE IS a baking sky over the yellow hills, and the air
shimmers. The bush is tinder dry, waiting for a spark,
waiting to explode.

Sweat runs into the typewriter. I can't think: the heat, the
jack-pump, the burning emptiness. And the freethinking,
unconventional woman hasn't phoned. Since Ingrid left, I've
been unable to work: I feel disoriented, confused.

I shouldn't have burnt The Book. Now that the
manuscript is destroyed, turned into ash, and the ash flushed
down the sink, I'm convinced that it was, after all, a work of
genius. There was a time when I thought that the whole world
was waiting for my book. The story of Mupp and of Adolf

Hitler; of mice in the park; of the charge attendant and Larry and Weston; of ten shabby men in the dock ...

I must reconstruct The Book. Suddenly, it's imperative that I reconstruct it. It was an attempt to make sense of my life, to find some justification for my experiences. I shut my eyes. How did it start? I try to visualise the first page. Words, lines, drift in and out of focus.

When he was two, he was given Mupp, a brown teddy bear with round ears and a round head who growled when he was turned upside down. Karl told Mupp stories. Mupp, who is almost bald, is still there and sits on the piano in the bedroom, straw poking through the worn soles of his feet. His nakedness is covered by a pink baby dress which Ingrid knitted for Helga.

If only Mupp had had a built-in tape recorder to record the stories he told Mupp so long ago. Mupp was with him in the bomb shelter and when the Russian shot up the room. They've been together now for fifty years.

The telephone rings, sharp and insistent, and I race to answer it. My pulse is hammering, and my breath comes fast.

A female voice, a voice I don't recognise – the unconventional woman? – asks for me by name.

'Yes?' My throat is tight.

'We're collecting for the blind ...'

'NO!' I scream like an animal and crash the damned thing down. How did they get my name and number? I'm not in the book.

I try Cynthia, my finger stabbing the dial. It rings and rings, but she doesn't answer.

I go back to the typewriter, but I've lost the thread. I can't go on. I press my fingers to my burning eyeballs. My head hammers. Cynthia! Ingrid! They dissolve into each other.

I wonder what drew me back to this place? These five barren acres, a kilometre from the town; the store and post office, a service station, the Uniting Church and the pub strung out along the rutted main street. I've avoided the townspeople since Ingrid left because I can't face the accusing blue eyes of Mrs Dugan, the postmistress, a broad, ginger-haired woman with freckled arms. I recoil from the exaggeratedly hearty greetings at the petrol pump from Johnno, with the beer gut and the red, glistening face and the enthusiastic, 'G'day!' I feel as distant from Johnno as from the moon. Did I really think that I would find a home here, grow roots and belong? Ingrid was the one who assimilated. I've shunned the church and the pub. To enter the church would be an act of hypocrisy, and I feel alien in the boozy mateship that binds the local men. I know they regard me as some strange animal, to be treated with courtesy but suspicion. I can see it in their gestures and their eyes. I wait until after dark to pick up my mail from my post office box and drive the fifteen kilometres to Mt Barker for petrol and supplies.

The heat was like this, baking, when I first stepped on Australian soil. The sea was like a sheet of silver. Gaunt cranes against a sky of dazzling blue. The air above the iron sheds swam like water and the heat in the ground burnt through the thin soles of my shoes. I was the little Jewish refugee arriving in the Promised Land.

I didn't want to be a Jew. Being a Jew was strange and somehow shameful, a terrifying apparition on a yellow poster: clad in a long, black caftan, with greasy sidecurls and a hooked nose, he swung the knout and clutched a sack of money.

The Fuehrer had seen to it that the Jew could no longer exploit the German people.

I start the tape. The voice of Adolf Hitler thunders, 'I will exterminate you!' *Sieg Heil! Sieg Heil!*

And when the Jewish blood runs from the knife,
We Germans will have twice as good a life!

I want to exterminate the Jew in myself.

I sat in the press gallery of the high-ceilinged courtroom in Cologne with a pad on my knee and watched the exterminators

7

in the dock. Otto Kaiser stood facing his judges and, beside him, seated, were the nine other accused, the once black-uniformed, jackbooted executioners of the Master Race. Ten shabby, bewildered men, wondering what they were doing here, twenty years after they drowned Jews in sewage, squirted them down and made them stand in the snow until they froze or hosed water down their throats until their bellies burst.

Ten shabby men, not in smart black uniforms and polished jackboots now but in rumpled civilian suits: a locksmith, a baker, an electrician, a mechanic, shop assistants, clerks. I studied their faces and their hands. They were faces that you see on the bus, hands that serve you across shop counters, that repair your car.

'My father was a communist.' Kaiser groped for words. 'We were all communists. There was no work. We lived in two rooms.'

'How many of you were there?'

'Seven or eight . . . I can't remember. My sister died. The flat was in the basement, and it was always dark. There was no work. My father was in the Red Front, and I joined the Red Front. They had a soup kitchen, and they gave you food, a place to hang out.'

'What did you do after Hitler came to power?'

'We were told there would be an amnesty for those of us who joined the SS. We were re-educated, given tough training to make us hard. They made us explode hand grenades on top of our helmets.' He raised his hand over his head. 'You can do that with a stick grenade.'

'And when you finished your training?'

'I was posted to the camps . . .'

The tall Gothic windows threw long wedges of sunlight on the floor. The court adjourned, and I left to file my story, but it didn't say what I felt. These men should have been hanged twenty years before beside the bodies of their victims. But they were not the ones who gave the orders; it seemed pointless to try them now. They would get ten years, fifteen, life, but in five years, all of them would be free, and they'd go back to their workshops and counters and tenement flats and ageing wives. Not one of the dead returned to life.

On the six o'clock news I watch Israeli troops blow up Arab houses. The Jews have learned well from their persecutors. A one-legged man firing an automatic rifle hops on his one leg; the other has been amputated at the buttock, his rump bandaged. He's in Beirut. But it could be anywhere. That pathetic, hopping and firing remnant of a man stands for all that is mindless and murderous.

A local item:
'Two male mental deficiency nurses pleaded not guilty in the Central District Criminal Court today to having assaulted a mentally handicapped patient at the Strathmont Centre last year.

It was alleged that the patient suffered extensive bruising to the groin area and that his scrotum had swelled to a circumference of 33 centimetres.'

I jerk the paper from the typewriter, crumple it up and toss it into the waste paper basket. I spin a new sheet into the machine.

    Weston bawled his head off because Larry lifted him off the bed by the balls.

Cynthia doesn't answer. Where is she? With the Reverend Christian Cleaver? At the thought of him my guts knot in a sick spasm of jealousy.

Cynthia swears that there is nothing between them, that Cleaver is just a sad old man, a rather ridiculous but devoted friend of the family who is useful because he runs her errands and fills her need for a father figure.

But I saw them through the parted living-room curtains, and their mouths were locked in a kiss that didn't seem fatherly

9

at all. I tiptoed away and waited, then returned and rang the bell. She introduced us. The Reverend Cleaver is large, with a large, pink face and a white, square beard and white, shoulder-length hair. He has a loud voice and wears a large silver crucifix on his chest. We eyed each other like fighting cocks. There was a little smile of triumph on her lips.

The phone rings, and I grab it. It is a woman's husky voice.

'Hello! Are you the writer? I got your letter in reply to my advertisement.'

It's the unconventional, freethinking woman! Her name is Simone, and yes, she would love to meet me, tomorrow night. She lives near the Belair Recreation Park and loves to walk. We could meet at the park. She gives me directions, and we agree on the time. How will I recognise her? She is of medium build – not too thin, not too fat – and has auburn hair.

My mood changes. I can see Simone: her auburn locks curling over her bare shoulders, the light in her eyes as she bends over me, her pursed lips, the tip of her tongue between her teeth.

I'll show Cynthia that she's not the only woman in the world.

I lie on my bed, naked, on a moist and tangled sheet. From the gully comes the sound of the jackpump, clunk, shriek, clunk, shriek, never missing a beat, monotonous, repetitive. I concentrate on the image of Simone.

3

MY LIPS AND FINGERS are red with blood, blood drips into my beard. I chew raw liver, half a pound of ox liver, bloody and slippery in my hands. I tear at it with my teeth, greedily, like a dog. I need energy and raw liver contains iron. Tonight, I'll meet Simone. It's boiling again, a hundred and six on the old scale. The liver is cold, straight from the fridge.

I rinse my fingers under the tap and blood swirls down the plug hole. The sink is discoloured, evidence that I burnt The Book.

I must do some work. I uncover the typewriter and stare at the keys. Yesterday I was interrupted; today I'm too tense. My moods swing wildly. Tonight, I'll meet Simone.

I remember a carton full of my old notebooks and old photographs that I put out in the shed years ago. Perhaps it contains an early draft of The Book. Is it still there, I wonder, or did Ingrid put it out with the rubbish? I must find it, now. I wrap a towel around my middle and put on my glasses. They hurt my nose. Cautiously I open the back door and blink at the glare. On bare soles I sprint over the baking clay. The shed's a furnace. I brush away cobwebs, move old bottles and gardening tools until I find the carton, which is full of shredded paper, scurrying silverfish. Cursing, I crush the squirming creatures.

I carry the carton into the house and upend it and kill more silverfish: squash them savagely under my thumbs, squirt them with fly spray. There are scraps of paper covered with my tiny handwriting, and a photo of myself at the age of nine or ten: a pinched face under a large, flat cap. The little Jewish refugee. The silverfish have scalloped the edges and eaten tracks across the image.

I didn't know that my mother was a Jew until after the war. By then I was eight, and I had been brought up to believe that I was a German like any other German. (The Jesuits say: Give us a child until it is seven, and it is ours for life.)

My father was an Aryan, someone who was not a Jew. The fact that my father was an Aryan, and that my mother had become a Catholic, saved her from a concentration camp.

The Jews are an inferior race, their Jewish blood defiles Aryan blood when mixing with it. The spiritual poison of the Jewish racial soul completes the act of biological destruction. If Jewish penetration of the Aryan world is not stopped, the end of occidental culture will

11

inevitably come. To rid ourselves of them is an act of hygiene, as a physician gets rid of bacteria.

When I was five, the Gestapo took my mother away. They came in an unmarked delivery van and drove her to Gestapo Headquarters in the Hotel Metropol on the Danube Canal. It was said that the bodies were thrown from the interrogation cellars straight into the dirty waters of the canal.

They questioned my mother in an office below street level. A man behind a desk ranted and threatened and called her a Jewish sow. Then she was taken to the cellars, beaten unconscious, and thrown into the street.

Her parents, rich Viennese Jews, had smuggled their property out of the country under my father's name.

There is confetti on the floor. My notes and The Book are destroyed. On hands and knees, I shuffle scraps of paper on the carpet, trying to fit together the jigsaw puzzle of my life.

```
     Weston bawled his head off because Larry lifted him
off the bed by the balls.
     'You're a dirty bastard, aren't you, Westie?' the
charge attendant said.
     Weston shouted 'WOW!'. His hands were locked in
leather muffs.
     The charge attendant pulled the dirty sheet
from under him. Larry whacked him across the belly
with his free hand and let go. Weston's behind thumped
onto the mattress.
     'You're a dirty bastard, aren't you?' the charge
attendant insisted.
     'I'M A DIRTY BASTARD!'
     'There, you admit it,' the charge attendant said,
in a tone that was almost kind.
     'That's a good boy, Westie,' Larry said.
     Weston grinned from ear to ear. 'WOW!'
     Weston ate his own shit and they called him the
dirtiest bastard in the ward. He had a big square head
that invited hitting, and they hit him all the time. He
```

suffered from a progressive deterioration of the brain.
Most of the time he masturbated, but if you asked him,
'What's eight times eight?' his face went tight with the
effort of thinking and he burst out with 'SIXTY-FOUR'.

And I stood there and said nothing. After my shift, I went home
to my ten shillings-a-week rented room and wrote about the
charge attendant and Larry and Weston, and Kowalski who was
an air raid siren, and Manley with his chess books and the holes
in his head, and Blum who starved himself to death, and Sir
John William Whitcombe. But nobody wanted to read about
them. Later, I wrote about other things, like the ten shabby men
in the dock of that German court.

I wonder if my preoccupation with violence is my Mars in
Scorpio, is it that I'm afraid of the devils that lurk in the depths
of my soul?

Mupp sits silently on the piano, his nakedness covered by
Helga's pink baby dress. I lift him up, and his glass eyes look at
me over his bald nose. Ingrid and Helga are gone, and Cynthia is
not here when I need her. Only Mupp has remained, my faithful
companion in all these years. Your once thick brown fur is
almost worn away, the straw pokes from the worn soles of your
feet. We haven't communicated lately, I've neglected you.
Once you shared my bed and I told you stories, whispered
childhood fantasies and fears. You listened and you
understood. My mother told me that a toy that is loved comes
to life, develops a soul.

I put Mupp beside the typewriter. He's mute. From the
valley, monotonous and unsettling, comes the screech and
clatter of the pump.

I stand under the shower and soap my armpits, turn the taps on full and let the jet pound my back and shoulders and rub myself down with the big soft towel. I gargle with disinfectant mouthwash, massage tonic into my scalp, roll on an underarm deodorant, sprinkle myself with a splash-on for men. I put on a clean shirt and the shorts I washed and pressed especially for the occasion. Scissors in hand before the mirror, I trim my moustache and beard. I squint at myself; I pass muster. I'm getting ready to meet Simone. I've changed the sheets and tidied the house. Perhaps I'll persuade her to come home with me.

The temperature is still in the high thirties. It's boiling in the car, and my back is glued to the vinyl. After the forty-minute drive, my shirt and shorts are soaked and crumpled. I stand in the dusty carpark and wait.

She's lovelier than I dared hope: auburn curls, a light summer dress that shows off her figure, tawny arms, smooth calves. She beams and my heart beats faster. I feel sticky and awkward. I smile back, a foolish grin. A man appears beside her. They link hands, walk to a car, get in and drive away.

I wait, disappointed. The crunch of soles on sand signals her arrival.

'Hi, I'm Simone.'

I turn. She is rawboned in jungle greens and combat boots, has a butch haircut and a large nose and glints at me through John Lennon glasses. She leads a large black dog that growls and bares its fangs at me.

She marches with giant strides behind the straining dog and drones on and on about the Peace Movement and the Liberation Struggle. I pant to keep up with her. Her body odour is pungent, rancid. Mosquitoes hum around us.

'Violence is not only permissible but legitimate in the struggle against oppression,' she says. Her voice is filled with religious fervour. 'Mao taught us that all power springs from the barrel of a gun.'

'I was taught to believe in Hitler,' I say, sadly.

Her glasses flash with indignation. 'You can't compare us with Hitler.'

'No. Hitler didn't spout false humanitarian sentiments.'

She responds with a venomous silence. We return to the carpark and part without arranging to contact each other again.

In the empty house a moth flutters round the light. Again and again, I try Cynthia's number.

I see the hated Reverend Cleaver, her Rasputin, the Minister of the Church of the Apostles of the Word, the meaty face, the white square beard, the shoulder-length white hair, the silver crucifix on his chest, his hunched shoulders, his great belly bulging above his tight jeans, the sixty-year-old religious hippie with the trumpeting voice. There is nothing between them, she insists. But I saw that kiss, and I burn with the green bile of jealousy.

I plot ways to kill him. I sabotage his car, see him screaming as he hurtles down the freeway with his brakelines cut, pumping the useless pedal and wrestling with the wheel as he crashes through the safety barrier and takes flight. I firebomb his house, stage a murder-suicide, shoot him dead before Cynthia's horrified eyes, then take my own life. But I lack a suitable weapon; my only gun is an antique flintlock. In perfect firing order to be sure – a great horse pistol that shoots a ball that will demolish a man's skull – but cumbersome and impossibly slow to reload: a dose of powder down the barrel, wadding, the ball, driven in with the ramrod, more wadding, powder in the pan. And then the thing may not go off. It gives a feeble sizzle instead of a bang. I would have to reverse it and use it as a club. Shooting a man is a different proposition to beating out his brains, even Cleaver's brains. I hear the sickening crunch of cracking bone as I rain down a hail of blows with the heavy, brass-knobbed butt.

CLUNK, SHRIEK, CLUNK, SHRIEK.

I turn all my fury to the pump.

4

I NEED a woman.

I have a desperate, burning, physical urge. Even the heat can't dull the knife's edge of my need. Like a caged wolf, I prowl the darkened house. The blinds are down, the curtains closed. The heat is stifling.

The male is a helpless plaything of his hormones. Nature pulls him to destruction by his prick. See the praying mantis, still rutting after the female has bitten off his head.

Under the white-and-blue striped skirt, Cynthia's pants, a little damp in the crotch, are printed with blue flowers. With an effort of will, I banish Cynthia from my thoughts.

Miscellaneous: Social and Matrimonial. I peer at the print six inches from my nose. Attractive young lady seeks generous businessman for fun times.

She probably has AIDS. Eighty-eight per cent of the prostitutes in Dar-es-Salaam have AIDS. I heard that on the radio. But I'm not in Dar-es-Salaam, I'm here in this smouldering heat.

The northern hemisphere is in the grip of the coldest winter in ten years.

In Vienna, the girls stand along the Karntnerstrasse between the Ring and St Stephen's Cathedral, or on the Naschmarkt, the old Sweet Market, by the Wienfluss canal. The cheapest are the Prater whores, who hang out around the amusement park with its huge Ferris wheel. In Berlin, you find them on the Budapesterstrasse and the Kurfurstendamm, in London, in a rough square bounded by Oxford Street, Regent

Street, Shaftesbury Avenue and Charing Cross Road, in Hamburg, in St Georg, behind the Central Railway Station, and in St Pauli, in the back streets between the harbour and the Reeperbahn, the glittering stretch of brothels, nightclubs, casinos and bars.

The time to have a whore in Hamburg is early on a Wednesday evening because they have their compulsory medical on Wednesday afternoons.

'Give me another fifty, and we'll do it extra nice.'

Promises, never fulfilled.

'Things will change.'

'You've said that for two years now.'

'There's nothing between Jack and me.'

'Then leave him.'

'I can't. Not now. He's negotiating a difficult contract. I couldn't do that to him now.'

'But there's nothing between you.'

'There isn't. But I owe him some loyalty.'

'What about your loyalty to me?'

'I love you. You know you're the only one I love.'

Her phone rings and rings. I smash down the receiver and drive my fist into the wall so hard that I shatter the fibro-cement sheet. My knuckles bleed.

The outburst has calmed me. I sit down at the typewriter.

    The charge attendant put a finger to his lips and
beckoned. He carried the loaded ear syringe. They
tiptoed to Weston's room and the charge attendant aimed
a jet of water through the peephole. Weston leapt from
his bed with a shriek. The charge attendant threw open
the door.
    'You bastard, Westie, pissed yourself again!'

And in the courtroom in Cologne, ten shabby, middle-aged men in the dock.

I turn on the tape deck.

Adolf Hitler.

There is only one law. Eat, or be eaten. We did not create the world. We must deal with it as it is.

I'm going crazy. I'm naked and blind. My world has shrunk to the darkened house, closed against the heat and yellow hills outside. But the heat still penetrates, the heat and the clunking and shrieking of the pump.

Finding balls and wadding and powder flask, I load and cock the heavy flintlock pistol and place the muzzle against my temple. My thumb rests on the trigger. One movement of my thumb and I will have wiped out the world. The temptation is almost irresistible. Instead, I turn the gun away from myself and rotate it in my hand; my index finger is now on the trigger. I point it and squint along the barrel, and the weight makes my arm quiver. I visualise the Reverend Cleaver – the long white hair, the meaty face.

A Chinese sage once said that every man should have fathered a child, planted a tree and written a book. I have done all three. But I have not experienced a fourth and vital act, an act the sage forgot. I have not killed a man.

Slowly, I lower the gun and place it, still cocked, on the table.

The keys of the typewriter are slippery with sweat. My ancient black Remington is as tall and heavy as a house: a transfer on the frame says SA POLICE TYPEWRITER No. 48. Once it stood on a police sergeant's desk. The stories it could tell of pain and passion and violence and death!

I reach for a new sheet of paper. My fingers leave damp marks on the virgin page.

```
AUTHOR, 52, recently divorced,
going mad, seeks lady
```

I x out the 'going mad'. I know that when I meet the woman of my fantasies recognition will be electric. She will heal my wounds and fill my emptiness, free me of Cynthia and Ingrid.

If only I can find the right words, SHE will reply. But everything depends on finding the right words.

My wrist brushes the pistol. I lower the cock and wipe the sweat from the metal with my handkerchief.

Adelaide, the City of Churches, is pretty between the beach and the hills. Colonial houses with iron lacework line its clean, straight streets. The ordered suburbs are full of neat brick-veneer homes with sprinklers on the lawn, a car in the carport, a rotary clothes hoist in the back yard.

But not all of it is pretty. The Pizza Huts, Kentucky Fried Chicken shacks, and used car yards make Main North Road and Main South Road desolate, dreary. In summer the heat shimmers over the roofs. On hot summer nights, the last trace of prettiness goes, and there's a menace in the air. Hoons gun their cars along King William Street.

I walk past the Town Hall and the stonework throws back the stored heat of the day. Outside the Criterion Hotel, a drunk argues with a cop. The cop's cap spins through the air, and the drunk lies on his back, his nose a bloody pulp. Two cops drag him to the wagon, fling him inside and slam the doors. The wagon speeds away. It all happens in seconds.

Adelaide is the city of disappearing children and bizarre murders: two sisters and their brother last seen on a suburban beach on a sunny January day, two girls vanish from a football match, five young men sexually mutilated and murdered, seven women abducted from the streets, their bones found later in the bush and on a rubbish dump.

I cross King William Street to the *Advertiser* building. It is nearly closing time, and there is only one clerk behind the counter. Nervously, I present my ad. His face is bland as he counts the words. 'That'll be seventeen ten. Will you pick up your replies or shall we post them to you?'

I continue on. The heat is humid and grabs me by the throat. I turn left into Hindley Street: the poor man's Soho or Reeperbahn. I avoid a gang of street children. A drunken Aborigine grabs me by the arm, but I shake him off. The police patrol in pairs with pistols on their belts. If there are girls, they're out of sight, in the bars or the back streets. Have you seen an ancient whore, all wrinkles under the pancake make-up? Hindley Street, tonight, is the wrinkles and make-up without the whore. Feeling bleak, I return to the car.

For a moment I'm tempted to drive to the block of home units in Plympton where Ingrid lives. Her place is filled with familiar things, the carved Biedermeier lounge suite, the prints that once hung on our walls, the china cabinet that contains the small gifts I gave her over the years: a miniature tea set, glass animals, a moonstone pendant on a silver chain. But she has withdrawn from me, erected a wall between us, and when a trace of the old intimacy returns she feels threatened and wrecks the mood by beginning one of the circular arguments that leave me angry and exhausted.

I head for the freeway, then detour south along Fullarton Road. Cynthia's house is dark and quiet. I suppose she's there, asleep, in bed with Jack or Cleaver. I can't see her car. I continue the long drive back to the hills.

The night air is heavy with the heat and still. In the gully, the jackpump clunks and shrieks, a focus for my aggression, my fear. My stomach quivers, my chest is tight, I clamp my hands to my ears, I scream.

I can't go on like this. I'm going to pieces. The gun lies on the table. It would be easy to end it all. I meant to create a paradise, but Ingrid left, taking Helga with her. The garden she tended has withered and of the trees we planted none remain.

I don't touch the gun but raid the fridge. Greedily, I munch slices of fritz and Kraft cheese, I spoon jam straight from the tin, and gulp lemon cordial. Eating soothes the pain. I sit down at the typewriter and stare at the blank page, then run back to the fridge. Later, I have indigestion. I twist on the tangled bed while the pump clunks in the valley. Cheese is bad for my sinuses, and I can't breathe through my nose.

5

THE SIREN HOWLS. A plume of smoke rises across the valley. The fire truck trails red dust along the winding road.

I shut the windows, pull down the blinds and close the curtains. I fill the bath and buckets and the knapsack spray. I raise the corner of a blind.

Again, I see the bright swirling orange of the flames. Ingrid and Helga, under wet blankets on the floor.

Attention! Attention! This is the air situation report. Massed enemy bomber formations over Carinthia-Styria approaching Vienna . . .

The bomb hit like a thunderclap and the bunker shook. The lights went out. There were screams and the lights came on again. The concrete had held: we were alive, unhurt. At the all-clear we ran out into the dust and the smoke. The tall apartment houses on both sides of the Barmherzigengasse were burning. We stumbled through the rubble, through craters filling with water from broken mains, my mother pulling me by the hand. We saw the twisted remains of a tramcar, and the blackened shapes that had been people inside. There was a huge bomb crater in front of our house; all the windows had been blown in, and the furniture, the walls, the carpets, were spiked with broken glass.

We huddled that night by candlelight while the fires glowed outside. The air was full of smoke and dust and the smell of wet ash and mortar, burnt timber and flesh. Lorries stacked high with wooden boxes containing the dead rattled over the cobblestones.

The scenes were to repeat themselves day after day. We lived without electricity or gas and queued with buckets for water. There was no more meat, no fresh vegetables, even potato supplies ran out. We survived on dried peas full of weevils and hard yellow bread baked from maize and sawdust. My mother ground up dried peas in the coffee grinder to make ersatz tea. Everything was ersatz, from the food to the cardboard soles on our shoes, until the ersatz, too, was no longer to be had. We became cave dwellers in the ruins, sleepwalking in a feverish dream punctuated by the sirens and the bombs.

'I demand that every German does his duty, that he fights and works to the last of his strength. For a people can do no more than that everyone who can fight, fights; everyone who can work, works; all united in common sacrifice and inspired by one thought: to save our freedom and our honour, the life of our nation . . .'

A poster appeared on the broken walls. A brownshirted hero, dead on the ground, a Swastika flag on an upright staff, torn by bullets but defiant. THE FLAG FLIES ON

I sing the Horst-Wessel-Song:

With banners high, in serried ranks and even,
The Brownshirts march, in steady step and sure!

The siren howls. A second fire truck churns up the hill.

Kowalski was an air-raid siren. Whenever a plane passed overhead, he howled into a bucket. It was the yellow plastic bucket he used to clean the toilets. He

stood on the steps, held the bucket before his face, and
howled across the yard.

They had to drag Kowalski to the treatment room.
Karl and Larry held him down while the charge attendant
wet his forehead, strapped the electrodes to his temples
with a rubber belt, and forced a bit between his teeth.
The doctor spun the dial on the little wooden box.
Kowalski gave a short, sharp scream, his face turned
dark red and his body convulsed. They fought him down,
battled with his berserk body until his frenzied
reflexes exhausted themselves and he became quiet except
for his chest, rising and falling, his lips sucking air.

The smoke drifts away. The fire trucks head down the hill. The
sky is bright, hard, blue.

I will not ring Cynthia today. I have advertised and SHE will
respond, she who will reconcile me with myself and with the
past.

From my speakers comes the voice of Dr Goebbels, as
hard and clear as glass:

'This is the last act of an epic, tragic drama. We must fight
and not capitulate, we must overcome all weakness and
indecision, we must trust in our good star and not show
cowardice to a mocking world. Instead of the white flag of
capitulation, we must raise the old Swastika banner in wild and
fanatical resistance, and thank God again and again that he has
given us a true leader in these terrible but great times.'

'Adolf Hitler, we congratulate you on your last birthday.'

My mother and I sat by the radio and listened to *The Voice
of America*. She had put a bucket of water against the door.
Listening to foreign broadcasts was illegal: the penalty
was death.

All day the German army had roared through the small
village near the Czech border in full retreat, lorry after lorry,

tank after tank, packed with soldiers who clung to every hand and toehold. They were young, boys out of school, their faces covered with sores from the dust and the lice.

When a lorry broke down, it was pushed off the road, and the soldiers threw away their equipment. Next morning the fields were littered with helmets, rifles and cowhide backpacks. We fired rifles, knocked the bullets from cartridges with stones and lit sizzling heaps of powder. We discovered abandoned field guns and an ammunition store. We loaded the guns with shell cases, empty but with primers that went off with an ear-splitting bang and a cloud of smoke. There was loaded ammunition too; we could have blown the village to bits.

I was at school – there was still school in Eibenstein as the world collapsed around us – when the news came. I ran to tell my mother.

'Mutti, Mutti, the Fuehrer is dead!'

Her eyes lit up. She said, 'Thank God, the swine.'

Two days of silence followed the German retreat. People spoke in whispers. I could sense the fear. And then the first Russians crept up the main street, pointing their submachine guns with round magazines.

An officer brought milk in a wine bottle for my brother, then a year old. I stared at the strange uniform, at the red star on his cap. That night, another Russian climbed through the window of the farmhouse where we had found refuge. He wrestled with my mother on the bed. She leapt out of the window. He fired his submachine gun and jumped after her. Flame stabbed at me in the dark, and my ears rang. My mother hid all night in the woods and did not return until morning. The walls of the room were pocked with bullet holes, there was plaster in my hair.

We were lucky. At the other end of the village, the Russians dragged the women from the houses, raped and shot them and threw the bodies into the river.

I needed my luck. They were all trying to kill me. The Russians, and the British and the Americans from the air. In Vienna, when the war ended in May 1945, the Nazis were building gas chambers in the parklands by the Danube for the remaining Jews and half-Jews.

The whole purpose of the war was to eliminate one little boy with a pinched face under a large, flat cap.

The telephone stares at me. No, I won't call her! I touch the flintlock. A ball three-quarters of an inch in diameter. What damage would it do to a man? I see the Reverend Cleaver's head explode: brains, bone fragments, teeth, hair, blood on the carpet and on the wallpaper.

What hold does Cynthia have over me? Is it her eyes? How vulnerable I am to her eyes. Is it her voice? Her eyes draw me like magnets; her voice, dark as her eyes, strikes a resonance deep within me. Does she look at Cleaver with the same eyes, speak to him in that same voice?

She was drunk when I first met her. Drunk, at a party, and she wanted someone to drive her home. I volunteered. I wanted to take her to bed. Most people become obnoxious when they're drunk. Cynthia drunk is euphoric; she walks on air. She wore a ring, but she had come alone. The Springfield house smelled of money, which later I was to curse. Without it she might have left Jack. She opened a bottle of champagne, although, God knows, she had had enough. She raised her skirt above her waist and danced while I watched, amazed and amused. I caught her as she stumbled. She clung to me and I kissed her – she tasted of champagne.

We were in bed when she told me about Jack. Jack was interstate; he was seldom here. She and Jack had moved worlds apart. 'My wife has made up her mind to leave me,' I said. It was the classic line, but she didn't question it.

Like Ingrid, Cynthia is a Cancer. I am Pisces, the attraction of two water signs. Cynthia's Sun is conjunct her Pluto conjunct my Pluto. Her Moon in Scorpio joins my Scorpio Mars in opposition to my Taurus Venus both square her Venus in Leo. An explosive combination: power games, violent passion. Am I obsessed with Cynthia because she is unattainable, because I know, deep in my soul, that she can never be mine? And while I chased the ideal love, a fantasy, I let Ingrid slip away.

All I have left are fantasies, terrors and obsessions. My perceptions have become warped, reflections in a distorting mirror. I hear the cold voice of sanity, urging me to wake up, but I cling to my delusions.

I look at the page in the typewriter. Kowalski is an air-raid siren. Few who went through it came out unscathed. Beside the machine, accusingly, waits Mupp. I must channel the fires that consume me into my work. I must reconstruct The Book. It was to have been my justification. I run a finger over the keys: thought fragments surface, then are sucked down again in the whirlpool of my mind.

I pick up Mupp, turn him head down and shake him. Once, he gave a rich, deep growl. Now there is only a loose rattle. I apologise and adjust his pink baby dress, the one Helga wore.

6

M ARS in Scorpio.

You are ruthless in action. You do not give way to anyone. Your determination is fixed. Your force is deadly. There are no holds barred when it comes to getting your own way. You sting like the scorpion. The position indicates strong passions and a tremendous sex drive.

The air is like glue, and sweat sticks to my skin. I run a bath, but the water is tepid, and I soak in a stupor. Lazily, my thoughts return to suicide: the stroke of a razor across each wrist, agreeable lassitude while the water turns pink, then red. The Romans knew how to live and how to die.

Is it true that the scorpion, when cornered, turns its sting on itself?

I was twenty-two and aboard the old P&O liner *Orion* on the way back to Europe when I nearly died. I shared a six-man cabin below the waterline, we were nearing the equator and it was hot, and I had lain on my bunk for days in a luxurious daze. I was dimly conscious of being carried on deck, before I woke in the sick bay where I was plied with jugs of salt water. A few more hours, they said, and I would have died of dehydration. I should have been grateful, but I felt resentment. I still wish they had let me die. Not that all that followed was bad; my best years lay ahead. But I knew that death would not offer me such easy passage again.

A passage to what? I wish that I could believe in an afterlife, that something of our identity remains when we die. But we are biological organisms, geared to survival in a physical world, the product of our instincts and our hormones. Strip us of them and what is left? Our passions rooted in instinct lift us to the sublime; the motor of our creativity. Could a eunuch have painted the Sistine Chapel? Written *Macbeth*? Composed the 'Eroica'?

I returned to Vienna. Fourteen years had passed. I left as the little boy with the pinched face under the large, flat cap and came back still not entirely certain of my manhood. After the sleepy country town that was Adelaide in the fifties, Vienna was huge, shabby, oppressive, grey in grey. The ruins had been cleared away, and new apartment blocks rose in their place, as grim as the old. On the Ringstrasse, rebuilt, the imperial buildings basked in their pretentious splendour, surrounded by hectares of slums. The people on the crowded tramcars were bad tempered and smelled unwashed. The Danube was an oil slick. The two flak towers still stood in the Arenberg Park, looming grey-green concrete bunkers that sheltered us during the heaviest raids. The words MOTHER AND CHILD were still legible over one of the entrances. I looked up at the platforms that once carried radar installations and anti-aircraft guns, at the bomb scars high above and heard again the howl of the sirens, the drone of a thousand aircraft, the thunder of the bombs.

The forbidding tenement in the Eslarngasse where I spent my childhood was as I last saw it, the same electrical goods shop on the ground floor, the same sour smell in the entrance hall. I stood once again in my old room with the green linoleum floor on which I played – how small it seemed. But the flat was warm. My father, still upright, witty, urbane, set up the chess board, and Resi brought Kipfel and Kaffee. The local Reuter office needed someone bilingual, and I was employed as a local staffer – less than a correspondent but more than a stringer. I pored over International Atomic Energy Agency press releases, trying to cull something from their turgid prose. I raced to the telex and fired off flashes and snaps when APA, the Austrian news agency, reported minor changes in the Austrian government. While I held the fort, my boss, a convivial Viennese, was out cultivating his contacts, an activity from which he would return, unsteady on his feet, in the early morning hours.

In those first weeks, I was terrified of putting one word wrong, that an error of fact, a misinterpretation in one of my stories, would have Kennedy or Khrushchev reaching for the crisis button. Soon I learned that the world cared little for IAEA handouts or minor changes in the Austrian government. In fact, I discovered that truth is a curiously relative thing. The truth was what happened to be on a piece of paper. Change that and you had a different truth.

I sit at the typewriter and search for the truth in my life, some meaning that will justify everything. The room is dim, the blinds and curtains closed to keep out the harsh glare, a brutal sun that burns the eroded ground to dust. Somewhere, a lamb bleats, again and again, mournfully, and the jackpump clunks in the valley. In two hundred years, the white man has ruined much of this fragile continent. I wipe the sweat from my eyes. I should install air-conditioning, but that costs money. And I wonder when the next fire roars up the hill, sending its blazing debris before it, if this timber, asbestos and corrugated-iron shack will survive. Will it survive until the rain comes?

In the half-light I squint at the page and chew my fingers:

```
He had an altar over his bed. The altar had doors
that opened to reveal a statuette of the Virgin Mary
holding the infant Jesus.
     He went to Bible school, where Father Schranzhofer
told stories and they sang hymns to the accompaniment of
his scratchy violin.
     He discovered a book on his father's shelves about
the Spanish Inquisition. A colour plate showed a heretic
burning at the stake. The picture haunted him through
the nights. If Christians burned people in the name of
love, then Christianity wasn't for him.
     Nazism was an honourable alternative. Nazism, as it
was taught in school, was all about patriotism,
community spirit, willing self-sacrifice, joyful
renunciation.
     They didn't teach that people were being gassed and
their bodies burned in ovens. They taught that Adolf
Hitler embodied the noblest aspirations of the nation.
     He put Hitler's photograph by his bed and placed
flowers beside it on the Fuehrer's birthday.
     The altar was stolen by a bomb victim who was
billeted in their flat, a thin, white-faced woman
who carried her belongings in a small bundle. He didn't
miss it.
     She didn't take the picture of Hitler.
```

I read what I have written, crush it into a ball, and toss it into the waste paper basket.

'There is no truth,' I tell Mupp.

'We all have to find our own truth.'

I look at him curiously. Did he speak? It is forty years since he last spoke to me.

'There was a time when I thought that I knew the truth,' I say. 'Everything was clearcut and simple. Now I realise that I know nothing at all.'

'Perhaps you have found your truth,' Mupp replies solemnly.

Mupp has lost none of his wisdom. It was my mistake that I ceased to communicate with him. He is the only one who listens, who cares. Cynthia is interested only in herself. Ingrid has left, taking Helga with her.

I must recreate my book for Mupp, who heard my childhood fantasies. I began by telling stories to my teddy bear, and I shall end, telling my story to him. Our story, for Mupp was there at the beginning, even if later I thrust him out of my life.

At dusk I drive down to the post office. There's a large brown envelope in my box, the replies to my advertisement. I feel the thickness. Is HERS among them? I resist the temptation to tear it open on the spot and, filled with a growing excitement, I accelerate up the hill.

There are seven letters. I look at the postmarks, the handwriting. One stands out, a generous scrawl on a blue envelope.

> *Hullo Author!*
>
> *I saw your ad and feel we may have several common interests, mainly books and language.*
>
> *Please ring the above number after 6pm any day.*
>
> *Sincerely,*
>
> *Patricia*

Short but intriguing. I slit open another. Carefully rounded script on lined foolscap.

> *My name is Carol. I am a divorced woman with two girls nine and eleven years.*
>
> *I would love a man to share ideas with, someone to talk to. I'd like a man with an easy going nature — not hard to get on with. I am not interested in discos.*
>
> *Love cooking and a little gardening. Animal lover. I am nearly nine stone and am five feet three inches tall, blue eyes.*
>
> *I've had too much hurt in the past and will be true to only one man and expect the same.*
>
> *I've heard of authors but don't fully understand it all.*
>
> *Oh yes, I'm a non-smoker — that is an important question I nearly forgot.*

I put it at the bottom. The next, in an upright, energetic hand, covers three pages.

> *I don't like pushy and judgemental people, dogma, fanatics, malice, gossip, superficial conversation, keeping up with whoever, singles clubs, being bullied or violated. I don't like lies or deceit, or suspicion, or jealousy, or being chained up ever mentally.*

Her name is Cheryl, a phone number. I read the others: a widow with two teenage sons, a divorcee who loves the outdoors and plays league ten-pin bowls, a telephonist into Chinese cooking, a full-time student of forty-two with three growing daughters. I strip and squat by the phone naked. I will start with Patricia.

7

I DREAMT of Adolf Hitler. It was a dream I've had before. I'm the little boy with the pinched face under the much too large, flat cap. I tug at Hitler's sleeve because I want him to love and accept me, to forgive the Jew in me. And I want to warn him, to tell him that if he doesn't turn back something terrible will happen. But Hitler is busy talking to his generals, too busy to take notice of a little boy in a large flat cap.

The dream pursues me through the morning. I see myself again as a six-year-old: Hitler's photograph by my bed, and a large, black and silver swastika in the cogwheel of the German Labour Front. My mother sends me to the shop with money and food coupons, and I buy the swastika with the change. The party is always selling things to raise money: badges, flags, toys. I feel guilty because I have sent the money without her permission, but she just looks at the swastika and doesn't say a word.

I didn't know then that my mother was Jewish, although she had become a Catholic, and that I was a half-Jew. I wanted to be ten so that I could join the Hitler Youth. The boy next door was in the Hitler Youth, and he looked very smart and grown-up in his brown shirt with the bright, red, white and black swastika armband on his sleeve and a swastika on the dagger on his belt. I wanted a brown shirt and a dagger too.

I found my tattered school reader in a stack of old books in my father's flat. It had escaped the book burnings, not those ordered by Goebbels, but of Nazi literature when the regime fell. I open it. Hitler's eyes stare at me, bright blue and luminous. I turn the pages. The story of a troop of Hitler Youth on the march – one boy's feet are so badly blistered that he can hardly walk. The troop leader says, 'We haven't much cash, but we'll get you a ride.' The boy with the blistered feet snaps to attention and throws up his right arm. 'I'll walk. *Heil Hitler!*'

Joyful renunciation. Willing self-sacrifice.

In the bomb shelter, a Hitler Youth gave up his bunk for my mother. He covered her with his own blanket. He didn't know that she was Jewish. Because she had converted and was married to a non-Jew, she didn't have to wear the yellow star.

It is past noon. The drawn blinds and curtains have kept out the day. I should cook some food, but I have no appetite, and, anyway, the fridge is empty again. Even the last piece of ox liver is gone. I live on countless cups of lemon cordial, which I sweat out in salty rivers as fast as I can drink.

In two hours I'll have to brave the blazing sun to meet Patricia. My date with Patricia has got me through the morning. The mornings are the worst part of the day, worse than the evenings when the clunk–shriek of the pump reaches a crescendo, when the walls move in, when I only want to flee. Patricia's voice on the phone was pleasant enough. She has read Miller and Mailer, plays chess, is a librarian. She is separated from her husband – they had no children.

With two hours to kill I uncover the typewriter. I've done no work today.

As a reporter he got out among real people, people of flesh and blood, to witness their everyday struggles, their defeats and their victories, their pain and their joy. On the desk he developed the editor's delusions of grandeur. The desk job insulated him from reality, allowed him to withdraw into a safe and comfortable cocoon of make-believe. On the desk, he was the spider in the centre of the web, he pulled the strings. Disaster or assassination, political drama or war, he played with them as with the pieces of a jigsaw puzzle. People and events were reduced to words on paper, the

human tragicomedy was judged on its merits as a news
story. It was easy to lose perspective. He began to
believe that he was God, that he was the one who was
making it all happen.

'The early sixties were good years,' I tell Mupp. Do you
remember the early sixties?'

'Yes, you were going somewhere.'

'I mean, the great figures on the world political
stage. Kennedy, Khrushchev, de Gaulle, Pope John the Twenty-
Third ...'

'And you were going somewhere.'

I ignore him. 'I remember Khrushchev in Vienna. In the
floodlit lobby of the Hotel Imperial – Hitler stayed there once –
Khrushchev shone, from the crown of his pink dome to the tips
of his gleaming black shoes. His fringe of hair glistened silver, he
wore a silver tie, and his dark suit had a silken glow. He looked
as if he had been polished with Mr Sheen. He was obviously
enjoying himself, basking in the attention and the power, the
ogre who had crushed the Hungarian uprising, who had banged
his shoe at the United Nations, who had come to Vienna to
teach Kennedy the meaning of fear. Compared to Khrushchev,
Kennedy was a little less than real, an actor in a Kennedy mask.
Years later, Kennedy was dead, Khrushchev deposed.'

'And you,' says Mupp, 'were still going somewhere.'

He is trying to tell me that I have a great future behind me.

She is not The One. I stand in the coffee lounge and look
around: it is definitely Patricia sitting by herself at a table for
two. She has recognised me from my description and smiles
expectantly. I join her, a little embarrassed. She is very slim and
has red hair, an aquiline nose and light blue eyes: an attractive
woman in her early forties, obviously intelligent, obviously

genuine. But something is missing, the chemistry isn't there. She is an Aquarian, her Sun in my Moon sign, an ideal combination. There must be other aspects, maybe the blocking influence of Saturn. I order coffee, we talk politely, intelligently, about books and writing, our travels, the difficulty of finding the right partner when you're alone again in your middle years.

She glances at her watch. She has a bus to catch.

'You have my phone number?'

I nod. We both know that we won't ring each other. 'I enjoyed our talk.'

She smiles. 'I enjoyed meeting you.'

I walk her to the stop. She gets on the bus.

I feel empty inside.

I'm back in the empty house. The night is sluggish, heavy and clinging. Moths shimmer under the veranda light and beat a tattoo on the fly screens. I listen to the high, thin whine of a mosquito. The jackpump. From the village comes the thump of rock music. It heightens the sense of dread that has accompanied me all my life; sometimes muted, low-key in the background, sometimes jangling my every nerve string, knotting my muscles, making the hairs on my neck stand on end.

I was always in flight, but from what? The bombs? The muzzle flashes and the hard, ringing detonations of the Soviet submachine gun? The Jews, strange and frightening in their striped prayer shawls, in the hospital at Hofgastein, who taunted me and threatened to circumcise me? The rocks hurled by the French youths shouting, 'Sales Boche', dirty Germans, outside the refugee camp near Compiegne? Or from the sadistic glee of the boys in the park when I was three?

The mosquito settles on my leg. I swat it savagely.

I always longed for a place in the country, for solitude. But even here, peace has eluded me. And Ingrid went. When I think of Ingrid now, there is a strange blank. After twenty years together, I can't recapture her face, her voice.

I haven't tried to phone Cynthia today. Why isn't she here to allay my fears? Because the Reverend Cleaver has come between us, the aged hippie with the shoulder-length white hair. Her Rasputin. My terror turns to rage at Cleaver.

This is crazy: an infatuation with a married woman who has another lover. My whole life is fragmented: I have no home, no faith; I am caught in a no-man's land between continents and cultures. Neither German nor Jew, not an Australian, my roots lie in a time of terror. Forty years later my life is still overshadowed by Hitler. Without Hitler I might have been part of Vienna's cultural life; my forebears, Jew and non-Jew, were actors, musicians, writers. But, for me, all continuity ended with the Third Reich. I was uprooted, transplanted. So I yearn for the father figure of Hitler, because, while Hitler was there, I still had a place where I belonged. I yearn for the destroyer.

We do not want our people to become soft but that they can be hard, and you, my German boys and my German girls, must steel yourselves in your youth. You must learn to bear burdens without ever collapsing, because whatever we create today and whatever we do, we will pass on, but Germany will live on in you, and when nothing of us is left, you must carry the flag . . .

'The worst thing,' my mother said, 'were the screams coming from behind closed doors. As long as I live, I will never forget those screams.'

When the Gestapo had finished with my mother, they threw her into the street. Someone called an ambulance and she was rushed to hospital. But she was pregnant and had a miscarriage. I would have had a sister.

My mother has become fragile and transparent, her strength turned to brittleness. It is as if a careless move, a loud noise, will shatter her like glass.

The pump clunks and shrieks. The throb of rock becomes louder. Fear closes in on me again, the desolation of abandonment. I pick up the pistol, pull back the cock, put the barrel in my mouth and close my eyes. With a convulsive effort of will I jerk the trigger.

I hear the flint strike the steel: a brief, sputtering hiss then nothing. I lower the gun.

It goes off with a dull boom and a flash of flame. The ball buries itself in the floorboards, six inches from my right foot. I stare at the smoking gun and smell the burnt powder. After an eternity, I can move again. I return the gun to the table as if in a dream. I kneel and touch the ball flattened into the timber.

I've escaped death by seconds of the delayed discharge.

My depression explodes into mania. No, I won't kill myself. I'll kill Cleaver. I've killed him a thousand times in my fantasies; now I'll translate them into cold-blooded action. Like Prince Yussupov, I'll rid the world of Rasputin.

8

YOU STILL hear it said that the German people didn't know about the extermination camps.

They knew, all right. My mother knew. Everyone knew. The word 'Auschwitz' was spoken in whispers. You were meant to know what would happen to you if you stepped out of line. But, you didn't, because the truth was too monstrous to grasp. So you knew but you didn't know, you didn't dare to admit the truth to yourself. The best kept secret of the Third Reich was also the worst kept.

Goebbels spelt out plainly what was happening to the Jews. His voice rings from my speakers, as hard and cold as ice:

'The Jews wanted their war and now they have it. But they are also experiencing the truth of the prophecy the Fuehrer made in the German Reichstag on 30 January 1939, that if International Finance Jewry should once again succeed in plunging the people into a world war, the result would not be the bolshevism of the earth and the victory of Jewry, but the annihilation of the Jewish race in Europe.'

'We are now witnessing the fulfilment of this prophecy, and Jewry is experiencing a fate that may be hard but is more than deserved. Compassion or regret are completely out of place. They are now perishing according to their own law: an eye for an eye, a tooth for a tooth.'

Goebbels, a Scorpio with Mars in Scorpio.

There were exceptions: we young really didn't know. We wanted to be invited by the Fuehrer to strawberries with cream. We wanted to join the Hitler Youth. We wanted to be soldiers and fight.

At the very end even children were sent to the front, then only a few kilometres from Vienna. Day and night, from the east, we heard the rolling thunder of the guns. The boy next door marched off in his smart Hitler Youth uniform. He didn't return.

By then, although the penalty for admitting it was death, even a seven-year-old knew that the war was lost. Most intelligent adults had known when Hitler drove into Vienna six years before to the cheers of the crowds that there would be war and that the war, like World War I, would be lost.

My father had known. He hated the Nazis. He was an actor and musician, and his friends were actors and musicians. He later spoke about the intellectual tyranny of the regime. Because he was an entertainer, he wasn't called up until the last days of the war. I remember him, pacing the flat and declaiming his lines, the chamber music evenings before the bombs ended everything; my father and his friends put their heads together and carelessly told crude and blasphemous jokes about the Fuehrer, in my presence.

'Hitler flew to Munich. The plane had no loo and he had to go. In desperation, he used his cap and threw it out of the window. When the plane landed, there was no one to meet him. "Where is everyone?" he shouted, "I'm the Fuehrer!" "You, the Fuehrer?" snorted a little old man who was sweeping the tarmac. "Rubbish. Haven't you heard? There's been a terrible accident. The Fuehrer fell out of his plane. They found his cap. His brains were still in it." '

It was dangerous to tell such jokes, more dangerous to tell them in the presence of a child.

My mother took me to the park. She shared a bench with a stranger who had the swastika badge on his lapel.

'I know a joke,' I said. 'Hitler flew to Munich and the plane had no loo . . .'

'Go and play,' said my mother.

'But I know a joke. Hitler flew to Munich . . .'

'Go and play.'

'My Papa told the joke . . .'

She took me by the hand and we ran all the way home. She spoke to my father, and I could sense their terror, more proof of the Fuhrer's power. You might joke about him, but the Fuhrer had clout. The whispered jokes were proof of that.

The German people today have absolute faith in the movement. They stand, I can safely tell you this, one hundred per cent behind us. Those who do not stand behind us, they are those elements whom we are now unveiling in the courts, they are the inmates of our concentration camps, they are criminals, convicts, ex-criminals and ex-convicts, they are a bunch of madmen, fools, idiots.

I fidget at the table in the coffee shop and glance at the clock. Cheryl, a Pisces, like me, is now seven minutes late. I doodle on my notepad. The blast from the air-conditioner has chilled my sweat, and I shiver. I find myself drawing a swastika, then another and another. The Nazi trauma; I can't free myself.

Ten minutes past the hour and she's still not here. Being stood up is one of the hazards of the meeting game. I steel myself for disappointment. Her letter: I don't like pushy and judgemental people, dogma, fanatics, malice, gossip . . . I had expected her to be disillusioned, bitter, aggressive, but the voice on the phone had a ring of laughter.

I've decided to give her five more minutes when she arrives. She stands at the door, hesitant, and our eyes meet. She approaches my table and apologises for being late. I hide the swastikas. She has full dark hair, dark eyes and a sensitive, open face. Her light cotton dress reveals soft bare shoulders and nicely rounded bust and hips. Her legs are a little too slim for my taste.

I listen to the chime of laughter in her voice. She's a social worker and has a twelve-year-old son who spends every second week with his father. Yes, the divorce was traumatic, she was glad when John left, but the period of adjustment was hard. The bitterness is there now, out in the open, then the laughter covers it up again; life must go on. She enjoys the theatre, concerts, sings in a choir. I tell her of the chamber music evenings in Vienna, my violin lessons, interrupted by the bombs and never resumed. She gives me her address, assures me that she has found me most interesting, and would really like to talk again. I promise to ring her, probably later in the week. But I'm not sure, she's nice enough, but something isn't quite right. Her legs? That we are both Pisces? Other Pisceans have usually disappointed me. Or is it the boy? I can't see myself ever comfortable in the presence of the boy. What would he call me? 'Uncle'? I was twelve when my mother remarried, and I vowed that I would never be a stepfather. No, she won't free me of Cynthia, of Ingrid, make me whole. We part with a smile and the promise I don't intend to keep. The heat is still scorching, and I drive home, bleaker than before.

Black depression. I fall and fall, down the bottomless pit. The wall rushes past faster and faster. I scream and claw. I must check my fall. I must rise out of the pit, for the pit is madness.

He reported at H ward. Pandemonium. The smell of phenol, sweat, urine and excreta. The old stone building was like a prison, the massive walls shut in the stink and the heat. Along the corridor, a row of heavy doors

fitted with peepholes, locks and bolts. He looked for
the charge attendant. He heard a loud crack and a naked
body flew past and landed on the concrete floor. The
charge attendant advanced with bunched fists. The body
on the floor didn't move. The charge attendant looked
worried, knelt down and examined the inmate's head.
Groggily, the inmate sat up. The charge attendant rose
and kicked him in the rump.

    'Get up, you cunt!'

The killing of Cleaver will have to be quick, direct, violent. I've
dismissed the more ingenious schemes: exotic poisons,
elaborate booby traps. Probably, the only poisons I can buy are
rat and weed killers, and they'd have a strong taste and I'd need
massive amounts. Then there's the problem of administering
them. Ratsack in his milk?

Arson? I might burn down the whole neighbourhood
while he escapes unharmed.

Sabotage his car? I'm no mechanic, I can't see myself under
a car with a torch and a spanner. Even if I did succeed in
interfering with his brakes, he could walk from the wreck while
half a dozen innocent people died.

No, the surest way is to wait for Cleaver on a black night
with a brick, a length of lead pipe, or a knife. Would I have the
stomach to drive in the knife, to batter his brains out of his
skull? When I tried to kill the cat – a car ran over it, and it was
glued to the road – I picked up a brick from a building site and
hit it again and again, but it kept on crying...

No, I need something that kills at a distance. The flintlock
pistol? Too unreliable. Something deadly but silent; a bow or
crossbow, you can buy them freely. Could arrow or bolt be
traced back to me?

They fed Rasputin poisoned cakes and wine, emptied a
revolver into him, tried to strangle him, but he still lived. Finally
they threw him, trussed, into the Neva through a hole in the ice.

Mupp sits in Helga's pink baby dress and looks at me. Will they let me take Mupp when they take me to prison or the psychiatric ward?

9

LIFE IS an accumulation of trivia, whether they bury you in a sack or in a marble mausoleum. We are specks in a test tube, bubbles that boil up and disappear. World War II killed fifty million people; now there are three billion more. The breeding and the dying goes on.

Whatever the purpose of creation, it cannot be our purpose. There can be no personal God. If he existed he would be a monster.

There was a nest of mice under the toolshed in the park. If you peeked behind the shed and were very still, you could see the mice scampering in and out.

One day the gardener was there, and the bigger boys, with a shovel and sticks, killing the mice. He burst into tears and his mother had to take him home.

Worse than the killing was the look on the boys' faces.

The round, shining eyes, the tight grins. Glee. It was my first confrontation with man's sheer delight in inflicting suffering.

Later I saw that look on the faces of the French youths who taunted and hurled rocks at us outside the displaced persons' camp near Compiegne. I saw it on the faces of the charge attendant and Larry when they lifted Weston off the bed by his balls.

'You're a dirty bastard, aren't you, Westie?'

'WOW!'

And I stood and watched and said nothing. Worse, I also felt that heady flush of glee. I was no better than they were. It frightened me.

Or had I learned too well?

The Jews in the hospital at Hofgastein grabbed my genitals and threatened to circumcise me. They were Jews from Eastern Europe, survivors of the death camps, debris, half-mad, terrifying. On Jewish feast days, they filed through the ward in a wailing, swaying procession, draped in their striped prayer shawls and holding aloft their scripture rolls.

I was in hospital for months with a fever that would not go away. It was 1946, snow lay on the ground, and the newspapers headlined Goering's suicide.

They moved me to a single room where the curtains were always drawn. I lay alone in that shaded room until I had hallucinations. The foot of my bed stretched and flowed until my legs were no longer mine.

In Australia, the Promised Land, my Jewish stepfather made me stand at attention while he reached out and struck me full in the face with a jarring hand. It was his way of meting out discipline. I took the blows, ramming all feeling down deep in my gut, determined not to give him the satisfaction of a flinch, or a flicker of fear or pain. Alone in my room, I defiantly stitched a giant swastika flag from scraps of cloth. He discovered the flag and ripped it to shreds. Again, I had to face his punishing hand.

Adolf Hitler killed people like my stepfather.

Yet, my great-great-uncle on my mother's side was Karl Kraus, writer, philosopher, critic of the decay of the Austro-Hungarian Empire, friend of Kafka and Werfel. I would have felt at home among the Jewish intellectuals of their day, stimulated by their humanity, their individualism and their wit. The Nazis, the war, emigration, have alienated me from myself and from my roots, I am a wanderer in a no-man's land.

Hitler killed people like Karl Kraus.

And I will kill the Reverend Christian Cleaver.

Why will I kill Cleaver? To win back Cynthia? Or from my need for purpose? The execution of Cleaver will give direction to my life.

Is the need for purpose the ultimate reason for war?

Of the seven who wrote to me I've met Patricia and Cheryl. That leaves Phyllis, Dianne, Cathy and the two Carols. The widow with the two teenage sons, the divorcee who plays ten-pin bowls, the telephonist into Chinese cooking, the mother of two girls, nine and eleven – 'I've had too much hurt in the past and will be true to only one man and expect the same' – the full-time student of forty, separated, with three growing daughters.

The telephonist? What's her star sign? She doesn't mention children. And better Chinese cooking than ten-pin bowls. I can't see myself suddenly surrounded by children, certainly not someone else's children. I've been through it all with Helga. But she's my own daughter and I love her, at least, I want to love her. I reach for the phone. I stop. I see ahead, the bleak disappointments, in the coffee shop, waiting, nervously fidgeting, watching the door, glancing at my watch and doodling swastikas. Is that her? The strained conversations, the hints of bitterness, of broken relationships, happiness passed by. I toss the letters back on the table.

I haven't tried to ring Cynthia for two days. I'm not her puppet, her helpless plaything. If she wants me, let her call me. What do I care if she has gone away with Cleaver, or if at this very moment, she is lying in his arms? I can see them: the meaty face and the square white beard, her eyes shining with that special glow, the wet communion between their lips and tongues, her greedy gasps as Cleaver enters her, her contorted features as he ruts like a bull, her legs locked round his fat middle, her fingernails raking his soft white back. Their hoarse screams as he comes in her.

It is hot, the vision has made me hotter, and in the valley the jackpump clunks and shrieks like a soul in chains.

'It won't be murder. It will be an execution.'

'You'll go to prison,' warns Mupp. 'Or to a mental hospital.'

'So be it. It can't be worse than this.'

'It can be, you won't fit in, you never fit in. They'll be out to get you, the other inmates and the guards.'

'I'll keep a low profile.'

'You will, in solitary or in a padded cell. You've seen what it's like. They'll stretch your balls.'

'Things have changed. Our psychiatric institutions and our prisons are civilised now, places of treatment and rehabilitation.'

'Haw, haw.'

'I can abdicate responsibility for my life. Let someone else take charge, do the structuring for me, the thinking, the worrying.'

'You won't like the lack of privacy. And the noise. They'll take charge of you, all right. They'll bugger you. Haven't you heard of prison pack rape?'

'I'm not beautiful enough for that, any more.'

'All cats look the same in a dark cell. But have it your way. Don't ask me to come with you, that's all.'

Even Mupp is thinking of abandoning me.

On the six o'clock news I hear that a former nursing aide who kneed a mentally ill patient in the groin has been released on a good behaviour bond.

I changed Weston's pants for the second time that afternoon. Weston said 'WOOOH' and pissed over my legs. Piss soaked my trousers and socks and shoes. I kicked him in the

45

shins. I kicked him again and again. He went 'OWOOOH!' and tried to draw his crippled legs up on the chair.

Larry and the charge attendant laughed as I hobbled away to rinse my socks and shoes.

I'm no better than the others. I can't sit in judgement over the charge attendant or Larry, nor the ten shabby men in the dock of the German court. I am planning murder.

In the dark valley there is a faint flicker of light, a spreading orange glow. A shower of sparks rises and drifts away. Fascinated, I stare at the spot. Now I can see dancing flames, I can smell smoke. Fire! The emergency number is on my phone. I hesitate. Will the fire destroy the cursed pump? Will it eat its way up the slope, growing, swelling, to engulf my house? The distant fire station siren howls. Someone has given the alarm. The siren is reinforced by another, drawing nearer. The flashing ruby light of the fire truck. The fire is a luminous pool from which sparks shoot like a coloured fountain.

I watch the firefighters, scurrying black figures against the flames, listen to their shouted commands. They have unrolled the hoses, and pump their knapsack sprays. The glow shrinks, fades; now there are only dying embers.

CLUNK, SHRIEK. The fire hasn't stopped the pump.

The fire truck is gone. I pull on shorts and shoes and find the torch. In the shed I search desperately, flinging aside wheelbarrow, boxes, tools. With torch and crowbar, I stumble down the hill. Now I'll silence the goddamn pump! I thresh through scrub, thorns tear at my calves. My feet slide, dirt fills my shoes. I trip, my outstretched arms break my fall, and the torch rolls downhill and goes out. Blindly, I crash on in the dark. Then sudden pain as barbed wire stabs into my chest. I lash out with the crowbar. The wire bounces back, gashing my arm. Cursing, defeated, I drag myself back up the hill.

Before the bathroom mirror, I swab away dirt and blood and dab iodine on my gashed arm and punctured chest. A blackberry branch hangs in my hair: my crown of thorns. All at once, I have to laugh. I double up and shake with laughter until tears stream down my cheeks.

10

OUR FLAGS were kept folded in the sideboard in the dining room. The flags fascinated me. On Hitler's birthday and other state holidays, my mother brought them out. Flagging was compulsory. Flags hung from every window, flew from the rooftops, streamed down the housefronts. Vienna was a sea of swastikas.

The sun was shining. The heavy raids hadn't started yet. My father took me to the Military Museum, the forecourt of which bristled with captured tanks and artillery pieces; a sentry stood on duty with a steel helmet and a rifle with fixed bayonet and inside there were uniforms of every design and colour, medals, shells and bombs, miniature battlefields in glass cases. A huge mural showed our soldiers in battle, firing rifles and hurling stick grenades. They looked heroic. We were given a brochure. On the cover was Hitler. Below it, the words:

I swear by God this sacred oath
That to the Leader and Chancellor of the Reich, Adolf Hitler,
Supreme Commander of the Greater German Armed Forces,
I pledge unconditional obedience.

I put the Fuehrer's picture on my bedside table. Because it was his birthday, I commandeered two of my mother's pot plants and placed them on each side.

The Fuehrer stared at me with those hypnotic eyes that had a touch of madness that touched some madness of my own.

When the Fuehrer's birthday came around again, Vienna was in ruins. And after the war, my mother made red aprons out of the flags.

'Mutti, Mutti, the Fuehrer is dead!'

'Thank God, the swine.'

The north wind flattens the yellow grass and threatens to lift the roof and tear the cladding from the timber and asbestos building. The air is brown with dust and the rubbish bin clatters down the hill. Will this year bring the third Ash Wednesday fire?

Whenever the fire sirens wail, I can hear the bombers overhead. But a bushfire sweeps past in seconds.

There have been two fires within two years, each on Ash Wednesday: the temperature gets up into the forties and the wind rushes at a hundred kilometres an hour. Ingrid left after the second fire; even Helga didn't want to stay any more.

Whatever made me think that Cynthia would leave the comforts provided by Jack to live here with me?

That any woman would live here with me?

The Jewish Nazi with the wild eyes and tangled hair.

The fire roared up the hill, a band of liquid red topped with a black wall of smoke. Ingrid and Helga huddled under wet blankets on the floor. I stood at the window and watched, mesmerised. If the glass had shattered, I would have been engulfed by shards and flames. Grass, bushes, trees exploded into swirling orange, and then the fire was past. I looked out on a moonscape of ... glowing embers and grey ash.

I stepped outside with the knapsack spray. There wasn't a soot mark on the house.

Ingrid had been convinced we would die. I was calm and detached. It wasn't until later that I felt the shock. For weeks we lived in that dusty world of grey, then the first green reappeared. Tender blades of new grass thrust their tips from the cindered ground and emerald clusters of leaves burst from the blackened trunks.

The wind batters the house. Dust swirls past the windows. The pipe that connects the gutters to the rain water tank comes down with a crash. I switch on the radio. Nothing. The power has failed. I pick up the phone, but the line is dead.

Now there is no running water. The house is supplied with water from the tank by an electric pump. I should get a petrol-powered pump and a sprinkler system. I haven't cleaned the gutters yet, or cleared around the house.

No phone, no power, no running water. And then the smoke, a wall of fire. But the house survived twice before, protected by an unseen hand. And while it stands I will be trapped here, tied to these five barren acres by invisible chains, like the Flying Dutchman, condemned to sail the Seven Seas until Judgement Day.

Only the unconditional love of a woman can release the Dutchman from his curse.

The rush of the wind sets my teeth on edge. I stand at the window and watch balls of grass, a rectangle of corrugated iron, hurtle past. A loose fibro-cement sheet rattles and bangs at the back of the house like a thing possessed. I should have filled the bath and the knapsack spray. Not that the knapsack spray is much use. You stagger along with the straps biting into your armpits and the push-pull pump straining every arm muscle, and you might as well piss into the wind.

Ingrid left after the second fire.

'You're crazy. A megalomaniac. Create a paradise in the bush!'

She lit a cigarette from the last one and crushed the butt in the ashtray.

The ceiling is still stained above the kitchen table where she sat.

'All I ever wanted was an ordinary, suburban home. An ordinary home, for an ordinary family, in an ordinary street, close to the shops and the bus and Helga's school.'

'But you loved this piece of land.'

'I always did whatever you wanted whether I wanted to or not. I always went along with what you said.'

'We discussed everything, we agreed.'

'No, you harangued me. It was always a foregone conclusion that you would have your way.'

'You wanted chickens and goats...'

'The goat and the chickens died. Like we nearly died. Do you want your child to die?'

Suddenly cut off, the wind stops. A moment ago there was still a howling gale. Now there is utter calm, an eerie silence. Water drips from the fridge.

I brace myself for the storm to resume in all its fury, but the silence persists. The radio and the motor of the fridge come to life. The power is back on.

I go outside to inspect the damage.

I haven't forgotten Cleaver.

Cleaver is a carbuncle on my back, psoriasis on my elbow, a worm in my gut. He is the personification of all I detest: the meaty face, the trumpeting voice, the hypocrisy and self-righteousness; a man of God who pursues married women; the fawning sycophant who runs Cynthia's errands, her 'spiritual adviser'.

Rasputin.

'I've told you, there's nothing between Christian and me.'

'You flew to Surfers Paradise with him. You told me so yourself.'

'We slept in separate bedrooms. Anyway, he's impotent.'

'How do you know?'

'He said so. That's why his wife left him.'

'But you go on holiday with him.'

'It was awful. He's like an elephant, always trumpeting and crashing about.'

'You speak of him with contempt, yet you keep him around.'

'He's useful. And he's a poor, lonely old man. Just look at him. He's so anxious to please. And now that he's retired, he has nothing to do...'

'For power and accuracy, the Barnett Trident.' Enthusiastically, the salesman removes it from the window. 'You have the choice of a forty-five and a seventy-five pound prod. Accurate to forty metres.'

He hands it to me, butt first. I aim the weapon. It is lighter than a pistol and a little longer, has adjustable pistol-type sights, a contoured grip and a safety catch. The bowstring isn't fitted, so I can't test the trigger pull. But for the close work I have in mind an ounce or two won't matter.

'Very effective for target shooting and small game. I've used it myself.' The salesman is a sporting type. 'You can fit a telescopic sight. I'm afraid you can't try it here. Too dangerous with customers in the shop. We haven't a firing range.'

'I suppose you could have a nasty accident.'

'That bolt'll punch through a car door at close range. They're banned in most of the other states. The big ones, of course, are a real weapon, as deadly and accurate as a rifle.' He points at a full-size crossbow that hangs among tennis rackets and scuba diving gear.

'Have you seen that Richard Burton movie, *The Wild Geese*?'

'The pistol crossbow will do me nicely. I just want it for indoor target practice.' I ask the price.

'A hundred and forty-five dollars. For an extra sixty dollars, you can buy a clip-on revolving barrel that holds four bolts.' He demonstrates the revolving barrel.

Four bolts, at close range, into Cleaver's chest. But I can't risk buying the weapon here, the man would remember me. People always remember me; it is one of my afflictions.

'Let me think about it.' I hand it back, and he returns it to the window. He looks philosophical about not having made a sale; it happens all the time.

I join the Friday night shopping crowds that throng Rundle Mall and make my way towards King William Street. I wait at the red light at the intersection. Before me, there is a familiar back: the hunched shoulders, the long white hair, Cleaver is standing on the kerb. It is almost dark, and people are pressing around us. Cars, a truck, buses speed past. Quick, now! I need no intricate plot, no sophisticated weapon. I must push Cleaver under the next bus, a sharp two-handed shove between the shoulder blades, then dissolve into the crowd and the dusk. The lights have changed, the bus has stopped. Cleaver hurries across.

Damn. I run after him, but I know that I've let the chance slip by. Where's he going? To meet Cynthia? He stalks down Hindley Street with his peculiar loping gait. People flood from a cinema. I've lost him. I look in shops and restaurants, search side streets. I've muffed it. Maybe it wasn't Cleaver at all.

A German march blares from the loudspeaker over the entrance of the Army Disposals Store, which is stacked with camping gear, knives, replica guns. They also sell pistol crossbows. The shop is packed with customers. The man behind the counter is wrapping a vicious truncheon for a

shaven-headed young thug with swastikas tattooed on his
biceps. This is a place where eyes are turned, no questions
asked. I line up at the counter.

11

The retreating German soldiers smashed the butts
from their rifles and threw them into the river, the
last act of the epic, tragic drama.
    He fished a rifle from a shallow spot. Even without
the butt, it was heavy. He carried it to his mother but
she threw it back. She said that the Russians would
shoot them if they found the gun.
    He had no hair then. His mother had shaved his head
because of the lice. He picked the lice out of his
mother's hair.

M Y MOTHER got dysentery, then I had a high fever, and
they took me to hospital, a crowded barrack where I
had to share a bed with another boy. He had a large head,
sticklike arms and a bandaged penis. My head was at one end of
the bed, his at the other. Our legs got in the way, and he yelled
when my foot hit his penis. He said I did it on purpose.

    The hospital was run by nuns in black with white starched
caps and white starched collars. They looked severe, and I was
terrified of them. Outside it was bleak, and ice crystals latticed
the windows, but the round cast-iron stove was lit only at night.
Our diet was a watery soup in which one or two small pieces of

potato floated, and I complained that I was hungry. A nun lectured me: they gave us what they had, I should be grateful.

I was transferred to Steinhof, outside Vienna, a lorry ride along a grey and endless road while the wipers beat at the sleet that whirled against the windscreen. Steinhof was once a psychiatric institution, but the mental patients were gassed by the Nazis. There was more food, and I had a bed to myself. In the mornings I could walk in a walled garden; the first snowdrops were coming out of the ground. The snow was thawing when my father came for me, and we journeyed back to the Third District by tram, past the gutted ruins of the Ringstrasse, the shells of the Burgtheater, the Opera House. A spring sun shone on skeleton walls and mountains of rubble.

My mother had left. The bombs had stopped, but the windows were still patched with cardboard, and the flat was sad and dreary and smelled different: my mother's smell was gone. Food was short again, and I queued for milk noodles with other children at an emergency kitchen. My father put me on a lorry and gave the driver a packet of cigarettes; there were tears in his eyes as he waved goodbye. I was not to see him again for sixteen years. The lorry sped along the autobahn to Salzburg, the seat was hard and everything rattled but the driver offered me bread and sausage. At the Enns bridge, the end of the Soviet Zone, Russian soldiers with submachine guns searched the lorry. It was nightfall and cold when we reached Badgastein, a Shangri-La of lights high in the mountains, but my mother was waiting, and I ate dried bananas from a CARE packet, the first time I had tasted a banana. I slept in a polished brass bed, between clean white sheets, in a room with a blue carpet and a view of the valley. Not long ago, Goering had stayed at the same hotel. Now the mountain resort was a refugee camp full of Jews waiting to emigrate, to North and South America, Australia.

Within a week I was back in hospital, in Hofgastein down the valley, in the ward with the survivors of the death camps, hollow-eyed and half-mad, alien, frightening.

The Jews are an inferior race, their Jewish blood defiles Aryan blood when mixing with it...
I WILL EXTERMINATE YOU!

I point the pistol crossbow and squeeze the trigger. Clink. The pull is heavier than that of a pistol, and there is almost no recoil. The bolt flies across the room to bury itself in the sack stuffed with newspapers, which I have propped up on a chair placed against the door. It has penetrated to the feathers. I clip on the revolving barrel. You still have to cock the bow and turn the barrel by hand, but the four bolts are in place and ready. I trigger them off, one after the other. The fourth thuds into the door, and I must work it free: I'll have to improve my aim and my dexterity. The hole is more than a centimetre deep. Solid timber. Enough power, surely, to pierce Cleaver's heart.

I loosen four more bolts, this time at point-blank range.

The phone rings.

'Hi.'

It's a woman's voice but I can't place it.

'How have you been keeping?'

She expects to be recognised.

'Fine.' My mind races. Not Simone. Patricia? The other, Sheila, Sherry... The one I'd promised to phone, whose legs weren't right, with the boy? I wait for a hint.

'I'm going out to dinner with some friends on Saturday night. Would you like to come?'

'Yes.' I've been taken by surprise. 'That is, I think I'm free.' I wonder if I really want to go. 'Can I ring you back?' I still don't know whether it is Patricia or Sherry, no, Cheryl.

'They're nice people. I think you'll enjoy it.'

'I'll ring you. Tomorrow.' Why doesn't she give her name?

'Right-oh. I'll be home at six.'

'Tomorrow at six.'

'Bye now.' She hangs up before I can ask her to give me her number again. Oh, damn.

The crossbow lies by the typewriter, cocked and loaded. I aim and send a bolt into Cleaver's heart. I've pinned a heart to the sack, cut from red wrapping paper.

The blank sheet in my old police Remington has a moist finger-smudge in one corner, but apart from the smudge it's as blank as my mind. I wander the room, touch the hole left in the door by the bolt, squat and put a finger in the depression where I dug out the pistol ball.

If the gun had fired properly, I would be dead now, my skull shattered. Is it luck that I'm a survivor? Others experienced far worse than I, but at least in the camps they knew who they were, who the enemy was.

My enemy lurks within me.

And I am still the frightened child.

'Speak to me, Mupp.'

He sits, in Helga's pink knitted baby dress, silent.

'Speak to me. You were there.'

Mupp's eyes are of glass; small, round, brown with black centres.

'You were there, on the train from Vienna to Eibenstein, remember? We hid under the seat when the planes buzzed overhead. They sounded like trail bikes in the sky, and the bullets from their machine guns made a noise like a bed sheet being ripped down the middle.'

Mupp declines to speak. He's taking his revenge for the years when I thought that I could do without him, when he was in mothballs in a dark suitcase.

Carol and I are in the coffee lounge, but we've run out of conversation.

She has told me about her church, her bingo evenings, her children and her grandchildren, speaking in a broad Australian accent, each rounded vowel drawn out. She has a round, nice face, a nicely rounded body – I'm drawn to slightly plump women with firm legs. I'm getting an erection; want to take her to bed, but I worry what we would talk about afterwards. She kneads her serviette, I stir what remains of my well-stirred coffee and surreptitiously glance at my watch. Another five minutes tick by, each minute an eternity. I pick up the bill, and we part in the street. She walks away, the late afternoon sun shining through her summer skirt reveals the outline of her legs.

As I turn the car homeward, I feel that now familiar low of disappointment that accentuates my dread, a flatness that gnaws at the bottom of my soul. I can't resist the urge to detour past Cynthia's house and park round the corner: the sun has set, the carport is empty, the house silent, not a light shows. I slip through the gate and stand on the lawn, the air is heavy with the scent of jasmine. I peer into dark windows, I listen. Is she with Cleaver?

Softly, I make my way to the back. The big bedroom window is dark. I hear the sound of a car, see the glare of headlights in the drive, and step behind the bushes. The headlights go out. It is Jack, the Media Executive, the International Traveller. He lifts a suitcase from the car and passes from sight. Lights go on in the house.

I'm tempted to ring the bell, to force a confrontation with Jack. 'Do you remember me? We met in the bistro at the Festival Theatre, some years ago, I think they were doing *Pal Joey*. Since then I've become your wife's lover. But she is unfaithful to me, to us. What do you propose to do about it?'

Jack looks at me, puzzled, then a shadow crosses his face. 'Come in. I think we should discuss this over drinks.'

I sit on the lounge on which we made love. Jack pours whisky and sodas, then pulls up one of the matching easy chairs to face me. I return his questioning gaze. I like his clear grey eyes and strong, open face.

'Another lover, did you say?' He twirls his glass.

'Cleaver.'

The grey eyes darken. 'The spiritual adviser. I should have known.'

'He betrayed your trust.'

'It looks like we've both been cuckolded, my friend.'

'Yes, we have.' He nods gravely. 'We must do something, mustn't we? Our honour demands it.'

'Our honour,' I agree.

And so we form an alliance against Rasputin, the unspeakable Cleaver . . .

I do not ring the bell. I sneak along the fence and tiptoe to the gate before sidling through. I begin to run. I reach the car.

'Idiot!', screams my reason, but the pain burns, unabated.

12

I STAND IN the dock and the charge is murder. Witness after witness points an accusing finger. The proprietor of the Sporting Goods Shop. 'He got me to take it out of the window, asked all sorts of questions, wanted to know, would it kill a man.'

'That's a lie!'

'The defendant will remain silent.'

The assistant from the Army Disposals Store. 'I remember him. He was furtive and nervous, sweating. Yes, I sold it to him. There's no law against it, anyone can buy one, they're quite legal in this state.'

Jack, self-assured: 'He claimed there was an improper relationship between the Reverend Cleaver and my wife. I should say that I have always held the Reverend Cleaver in very high esteem, a trusted friend of the family, our spiritual adviser. He tried to incite me to participate in some bizarre plot against Cleaver.'

'You rejected his suggestions?'

'I laughed in his face.'

Cynthia, prim in a high-necked buttoned blouse, her hair pinned tightly back, austere, has just the right tremor of indignation in her voice.

'The Reverend Cleaver was like a father to me, to the whole family: he baptised our children, helped us to find strength in our faith in times of trouble.'

'Do you deny any improper relationship between yourself and the Reverend Cleaver?'

'I most strongly deny it.'

'And between yourself and the defendant?'

'The defendant had some kind of obsession about me which I neither encouraged nor returned. I had to ask Jack to change the locks. I told Jack to throw him out if he continued to turn up at the house uninvited.'

My psychiatrist: 'I have numbered the defendant among my patients for some ten years. He has a strange identification with Hitler, and with Prince Yussupov, the Russian noble who helped murder Rasputin. My diagnosis is that he is a schizoid paranoiac with anal obsessive tendencies and a manic depressive psychosis. Yes, this man is dangerous, both to himself and to the public.'

'Ladies and gentlemen of the jury, do you find the defendant guilty as charged?'

'We find the defendant not guilty by reason of insanity.'

'It is the ruling of this court that the defendant be taken to a high-security psychiatric institution and there be kept until the Governor's pleasure be known.'

'OWOOOH!' Larry and the charge attendant are lifting me off the bed by my balls.

'OWOOOH!' I kicked Weston again and again. And Larry and the charge attendant laughed.

I went home, to my ten shillings-a-week rented room, and wanted to write about the charge attendant, and Larry, and Sir John William Whitcombe, and Blum, who starved himself to death, but I felt sick.

Kicking Weston felt good.

It was the day before my twenty-first birthday. Where was the child who wept when the big boys killed the mice?

Killing Cleaver will feel good, even if the charge is murder.

I lie on the damp and twisted sheet, gripped by a sense of dread so terrifying and oppressive that it threatens to crush me. It is nearly noon: the gap below the blind is a dazzling bar of light, but the rest of the room is dark. Outside, the hard sun blazes down on the glowing iron roof and the yellow grass and the dust. I twist and cover my eyes to escape the band of glare, open my mouth to scream, but the pillow swallows my cry of pain and despair.

It is the insistent jangle of the phone, distant at first in my hazy consciousness, then intruding with a rising urgency, that jars me out of my paralysis and sends me stumbling along the passage. My hand is on the receiver when the ringing stops. I dial, fumble, disconnect and dial again.

'Yes?' A deep male voice. I forgot that Jack has returned. I put down the phone. From the chair by the door, the Reverend Cleaver leers at me, the stuffed sack of a body, the red paper heart pierced by four bolts. I've added a head: eyes, nose, beard, long hair, textad crudely on a brown paper bag. With all my strength, I drive my fist into Cleaver's newspaper-filled belly. The paperbag head topples to the floor. I jerk a brass-tipped bolt out of Cleaver's chest. With the bolt in my fist, I stab at Cleaver again and again in savage fury.

I fling open the phone book. Only four Cleavers are listed, and none with the initial C. I find the Church of the Apostles of the Word.

'Are you sure he's with our church?'

'I think he's retired now.'

'One moment.' A pause. 'He could be in our retirement home in Fullarton. I'll give you the number.'

A retirement home. Damn! That'll make things more difficult. In Fullarton. A short drive to Springfield. I write down the phone number.

'May I have the address?'

'14a Launder Avenue.'

I thank him. I ring the retirement home and ask for Cleaver.

'I'm afraid the Reverend Cleaver isn't in.'

'Do you know when he'll be back?'

'I don't know. Who's speaking?'

'I was a member of his congregation.'

'I'm sorry. He's been away for several days.'

And Jack is back alone. I knew it. Cleaver is with Cynthia! Or is he? I must have proof. I circle the telephone. I steel myself and again dial Cynthia's number.

Jack's voice. 'Yes?'

'May I speak to Cynthia, please?'

'Who is it?'

'I'm a friend of Pauline's.' Cynthia sometimes mentioned a Pauline.

'I don't believe I know her.'

'Pauline's inviting a few friends to dinner. We wondered if Cynthia would like to come.'

'Cynthia isn't here.'

'When will she be back?'

'I don't know.'

'Can you tell me where we can contact her?'

'I'm afraid I can't.'

The suspicious husband? The husband who doesn't know where his wife is? Or who knows only too well and doesn't like it?

Jack is still on the line, not saying anything, waiting. I will have to be the one to end the conversation. Should I mention Cleaver? I decide not to. 'Thank you. Give Cynthia my regards. Our regards, Pauline's.'

Silence.

'Goodbye.'

Silence.

I hang up. Jack's behaviour on the phone was definitely strange. Maybe he recognised my voice and wasn't fooled. Perhaps he is suspicious of all male callers who ask for Cynthia. But, and that is the most likely, my call has touched a raw nerve. Jack knows where she is. With Cleaver.

Clink. I send a bolt into Cleaver's heart.

Paralysis. Cleaver is away, and there is nothing I can do but wait; my hands are tied. I prowl the prison of my house, every nerve aquiver. My powerlessness returns and, with it, the dread. I fight my dread with compulsive eating: I shun regular meals, and raid the fridge to chew hunks of fritz, processed cheese, raw liver; I spoon jam from the tin, scoop handfuls of biscuits from the jar I keep on top of the kitchen cupboard. I push the jar to the back, out of reach, then climb a chair to grab another biscuit. Only yesterday I drove the thirty kilometres to Mt Barker and back for supplies, and already I'm almost out of food. I suffer from chronic indigestion, my belly is bloated. I circle the table where my typewriter waits. Biscuit crumbs fall from my beard.

'Write your book,' says Mupp, 'and forget this destructive obsession with Cynthia and Cleaver.'

So he has decided to speak to me again.

'You wrote that great book, remember? The book that the whole world was waiting for, about me, Mupp, and about

Adolf Hitler, about the charge attendant and Larry and the ten shabby men in the dock, and Blum, who starved himself to death. And then you burnt it.'

'Maybe that was all it was good for. Burning.'

'You didn't think so at the time you wrote it.'

'Who wants to read about another teddy bear? We've had Aloysius. Who wants to read about Hitler, or the ten men in the dock, or the charge attendant and Larry? All that was years ago. Who cares? It's all been done to death. Who wants to read about the little boy with the pinched face under the ridiculous, large flat cap?'

'I'm sure they'll want to read about me,' Mupp says in a huff.

'Millions of children are starving in Africa. And they've never even seen a teddy bear.'

From the radio I learn that terrorists have lobbed hand grenades into a crowded restaurant in Paris, or was it Rome? Eighteen people are dead, dozens are injured. A rightwing political organisation has claimed credit for the attack.

    Blum starved himself to death...

A news update. The death toll from the terrorist attack in Paris, or was it Rome, has risen to twenty-one.

It is almost dark and still oppressively hot. My shirt is wet on my back and below my armpits; I can feel a ring of sweat under the tight waistband of my soggy shorts. I stand in Launder Avenue and peer over the hedge of 14a. The retirement home of the Church of the Apostles of the Word is an old, single-fronted bluestone cottage on a deep, narrow block, typically

Adelaidean, with iron lacework on the verandah. A lane runs along one side. I follow the lane, between galvanised-iron fences, to another lane at the back. The house has been extended, a modern addition of cream brick with a carport at the rear. Access to the carport is from the back lane, through a gate in the new, shiny fence. The gate is chained and padlocked.

Cleaver has a car, he must use the back gate. He must leave the car to unlock, or to lock, the gate. I judge where he would stop the car, the position of the driver's side door, my best vantage point. The moment to catch him is when he returns home. I must wait here, around the corner, out of sight. When he opens the car door, the inside light will go on, and he will be in the light and I in the dark. I'll take two steps and aim the bow just as he turns in his seat to get out, at a disadvantage, exposing his chest. Clink! right in the heart.

13

Blum starved himself to death...

THE SAME SENTENCE sitting unfinished in the typewriter since yesterday. I try to think.

Blum starved himself to death. He had a number tattooed above his left wrist. Before he died, he looked like one of the corpses at Auschwitz, all skull and ribcage and hollows; his sinews stood out like cords.

He starved himself with great determination. When they force-fed him, he retched and retched until it all came up again. They waited for him to die. At the end, he weighed almost nothing: you could feel his spine when you put your hand on his shrunken belly. His back was

one great bedsore; raw, pink flesh where his shoulder
blades had worn through the blue-black skin. And all the
time, he looked about him with a kind of wonder, with
brown, childlike eyes.

Why did Blum choose to end his life like this, to complete the
work of the Nazi extermination machine? I wonder if it was a
conscious decision, whether he was unable to cope with
liberation and its aftermath, unable to take root in strange soil.
Perhaps his terror never ended, he was still in Auschwitz, or
Sobibor, or Treblinka, or perhaps he had simply drifted away,
into a new dimension.

Or did he want to kill the Jew in himself?

When Blum was dead, they took off his bed jacket,
which reached only to his navel, tied up his penis and
plugged his anus with cotton wool. He lay on the
barouche, tightly wrapped on a white shroud, a nametag
pinned to his feet.

The Sheriff talked to himself and took swinging strides as we
coasted the barouche along the path, making the body roll on
the canvas. He was huge and on his shirt was a cardboard star.
The greasy old hat on his head bulged because he kept his
collection of cowboy comics in it, jammed into the crown. The
Sheriff had no respect for the dead.

The morgue was a small brick building. In a bare, dim
room there were two long tables and we lifted Blum onto one of
them. I measured him for his coffin with a long wooden rule
and switched on the ventilator. It was Friday night and the
temperature was still in the high nineties; we would have to put
wet sheets over Blum every few hours until the undertaker
collected him on Monday.

'Oh, the old grey mare she ain't what she used to be,'

65

crooned the Sheriff, 'ain't what she used to be ...'

I took the Sheriff to the boiler room to feed the hot water furnace. I watched as he thrust the shovel into the coal heap; he looked as strong as an ox as he pitched the coal, shovelful after rasping shovelful, in the red glow of the fire, grunting and mumbling to himself. He had killed his brother with an axe.

'Oh, the old grey mare she ain't what she used to be, many long years ago-o-o!'

I grope my way about the house, naked and without my glasses, in a blur, only the pictures, memories, fantasies, illusions, are vivid and in focus. The fridge is empty again, no milk, no eggs, the last traces of margarine in a plastic container, no bread. Maybe I should go back to bed, turn my face to the wall like Blum, and switch on the pictures, see them projected on the white wall or inside my eyelids, watch them as I drift away in pleasant euphoria with no one to drag me back as they dragged me back on the *Orion*.

Now I have let everything slip away – my marriage, my career – and Cynthia has deserted me.

The best year was after I came back, no, it was those three short months, on the Murray. The river was magic and Ingrid was loving and Helga was taking her first hesitant steps. The shack had no fly screens, a yellow wasp with a black-banded belly buzzed in and out to build its nest on the back of the food-safe, and a blue-tongue lizard lived under a rock below the window. It was Christmas, then New Year; and we spent the days lazing, watching the pelicans soar past. We walked in the burnished copper sunsets when the snakes basked on the rocks. At night, frogs with suction-cup toes glued themselves to the window panes to gobble moths, drawn by the light, with bright curtain patterns on their wings. When we lay in the dark under our mosquito nets, we heard the soft plop of the frogs on the floor and the symphony of night creatures in the reeds.

'It's Ingrid, not Cynthia, you're really grieving for,' says Mupp.

'Ingrid left.'

'And you're always moaning how Cynthia deserted you.'

I want to hit him.

'What's the power that Cynthia has over you, anyway?'

'Samantha says she appeals to my Grand Water Trine.'

'The astrologer! What she appeals to is your masochism. Samantha also said that her Sun is conjunct Pluto. Cynthia is a manipulator. For her, love is power.'

'When she looks at me in that special way with her dark eyes large and moist and shining, when she whispers to me in that voice, she makes me feel that I'm the only man on earth. I walk ten feet tall.'

'You've seen her use that look on others.'

'But I'm the one she loves.'

'That's what she tells you. What about Cleaver?'

Again I want to hit him, to send him spinning across the room, pink baby dress and all, but I restrain myself. He stares at me with his round glass eyes.

'Do you think that, if she were free, she would marry you, that you could live with her and her demands? You know she is fickle, selfish, unreliable, unfaithful. She could never make you happy.'

'Perhaps I need to be in love with her. Not being in love with her would leave too great an emptiness.'

'You're still in love with Ingrid.'

'Am I?' There is a chasm between us now. We met in the street quite by chance; I was hurrying across Victoria Square to catch the Glenelg tram, and there she was, coming towards me; I don't know who saw the other first. We stopped by the fountain, and, for a moment, at that instant of recognition, I felt the old pleasure, and saw it mirrored on her face. We greeted each other in the old, familiar way, *'Taube!'* *'Hase!'* I wanted to embrace her, and I think she wanted to embrace me. And then, like a curtain coming down, her face blanked out, she became distant, formal. She was late for an appointment – she did not say where – I had to catch my tram. We hurried in opposite directions. Afterwards I felt an acute sense of loss.

The clunk and shriek of the pump is eerie, threatening. The pump and the heat. What day is it? Saturday? I could have gone out to dinner with Cheryl and her friends. Or was it Patricia?

I don't ring either Cheryl or Patricia. Instead I prowl my prison.

With a table knife I pack wood filler into the hole in the door left by the bolt. They mustn't find the hole. When the deed is done, I'll have to dispose of the weapon: the little crossbow should be easy to get rid of, easier than a gun. The frame is of aluminium. It would be a simple matter to cut it up with a hacksaw and to bury the pieces in the bush. Will the man in the Army Disposals Store remember me? It was careless, and foolish too, to have called the church, to have gone to Launder Avenue. Someone will remember the calls, my accent, someone will have seen me creeping round the house, but how else can I find out whether Cleaver has returned?

I smooth the filler with the knife – a dab of paint and the spot will be invisible. Mupp watches me with his round eyes.

By the typewriter lies the crossbow, four more bolts in the barrel. I must work on The Book. Instead, I draw eyes, disembodied, staring eyes. I cover sheets of paper with patterns of staring eyes.

Big Brother eyes, watching me. The eyes of Adolf Hitler.

I can't free myself from the Great Destroyer.

I envy those who have faith. Those who can throw up their right arm or sink to their knees in fanatical fervour.

I believe in nothing, so I must take full responsibility for my actions. After I kicked Weston, I was sick in my gut because my only justification was that it made me feel good. I wonder if I'll be sick in the gut after I murder Cleaver.

I have to murder Cleaver. My hatred of Cleaver and my

determination to kill him are all I have left to give purpose to my life.

My hatred of Cleaver, and The Book. The Book: a blank sheet waiting in the typewriter; while I cover pages of clean white paper with Hitler's eyes.

I believe in nothing, and I am not free.

14

I KNOW THAT I will go to prison or to a psychiatric ward. They will come for me in the dark hour before the sun climbs, hard and bright, over the hill. They will leave their cars out of sight, beyond the bend in the dusty road, and swarm stealthily up the rise to surround the house, pointing their pistols and shotguns through the bushes. And then, the voice through the loud hailer, martial, will boom, 'We know you're in there. Come out quietly with your hands above your head.' I'll hear the crash of the door, kicked in, the snap of steel around my wrists, feel their rough hands on me as they bundle me away to the waiting cell. But they will be my liberators; they will have freed me from a far worse prison.

I pace my cage, around me dead and useless objects, my silent keepers: books, unread or read and forgotten, records no longer played – I can't concentrate on music – knick-knacks and souvenirs once greedily acquired. In the wardrobe are the suits I bought in the sixties, narrow-lapelled, the trousers too tight in the waist, the narrow ties, a little greasy. I pull open a drawer: discarded spectacle frames, ballpoints that no longer write, a fountain pen with a crossed nib, pencil stubs, a pocket knife with a broken blade, a single cuff link, the wrist watch that has not kept time for years, worthless coins: German pfennigs, Austrian groschen, Yugoslav paras, an unused 1984 pocket diary, the year that Ingrid left. I don't know why I hoard this junk; I burnt my notes, The Book.

Prison reduces you to essentials, breaks the tyranny of objects. Even the clothes on your back are not your own.

Prison, or the psychiatric ward.

They drew the bolts and turned the keys and the patients came tumbling naked out of their rooms (they were instructed not to call them cells), each room six feet by eight, just big enough for the iron bed and a wooden chair. A table in the corridor was heaped with clothing. They handed out work shirts as stiff as boards, moleskin pants, rough brown jackets, lumpy woollen socks and old army boots without laces. The patients had to take what they were given, trousers too tight to be buttoned or too loose, and they shuffled about in their Chaplinesque laceless boots, holding their pants up.

' "Thou shalt not commit adultery!" ' I shout at Cleaver. ' "Thou shalt not covet thy neighbour's wife!" You call yourself a man of God, don't you know Proverbs 6:23-33? You bloody hypocrite, you fornicating bastard! In a society less soft than ours, in a society with some values, you'd be stoned!'

He sits there, on his chair by the door, with his paperbag head and newspaper-stuffed sack of a body. The pierced heart on his chest makes him look like the suffering Christ in a Roman Catholic painting.

'In killing you, I shall be dispensing biblical justice.'

' "Let him who is without sin cast the first stone," ' says Mupp. 'Anyway, he can't hear you.'

I turn on Mupp. 'You can hear me, so why shouldn't he? What's so different between you? He's stuffed with back copies of the *Advertiser*. You're stuffed with straw.'

'Your love gave me a soul. When you still loved me, that was. You did love me once. You were nicer then.'

'My hatred gives him a soul.'

'Hatred destroys the soul.'

'I want to destroy him.'

'It is your soul you are destroying, not his.'

'Maybe I want to destroy myself, too.'

```
He had to shave ten patients with one razor blade.
They began to yell and the blood started to flow. He
asked the charge attendant for a new blade. The charge
attendant unscrewed the razor, took out the blade and
whetted first one edge and then the other on the
tablecloth. 'Now it'll shave another ten.'
```

I must know if Cleaver has returned. No, I can't risk calling the rest home too often. Another trip to Launder Avenue to see if his car is there. Is Cynthia back? If they went away together, he should be back too. I dial Cynthia's number, ready to hang up if Jack answers. Nobody there.

Can I disguise my voice? They've developed a gadget now that makes your voice unrecognisable over the phone. I put a blank tape in the deck and plug in the mike. I have no sophisticated equipment: no computer speech synthesiser kit nor band pass filters, no graphic equaliser. But I can play with the treble and bass.

'May I speak to the Reverend Cleaver?' I repeat it, varying the pitch, now shrill, now low, now holding my nose. I play it back; it still sounds like me. I try again, drawing out my vowels in Australian broad. I attempt a quavering falsetto and boost the treble and cut the bass. That's better. I record the sentence several more times before I'm satisfied.

The thin, shaky voice of an old woman. 'May I speak to the Reverend Cleaver?' Then, in case I'm asked who's calling, 'Mrs Beazley, Mrs Cecilia Beazley.' A convincing name for one of Cleaver's elderly former parishioners. Mrs Beazley would end the call politely, 'Thank you.'

I rewind, play it back and adjust the volume. 'May I speak to the Reverend Cleaver ... Mrs Beazley, Mrs Cecilia Beazley ... thank you...' I rewind. I carry the phone to the speaker and ring the rest home. If Cleaver answers, I'll disconnect.

'Who's there?' A voice, but it's not Cleaver's.

I press play. 'May I speak to the Reverend Cleaver?' I press pause.

'Sorry, he isn't here.'

He doesn't ask who is calling. I restart the tape, clamping my hand over the mouthpiece so that he cannot hear the 'Mrs Beazley,' remove my hand for the 'Thank you' and hang up.

I must record one more sentence. 'When will he be back?'

```
    They wheeled the food from the kitchen in big metal
containers: thick gruel soup, a stew with potatoes or
cabbage and, for dessert, yellow custard and red jelly.
There were not enough mugs for the soup, so some
patients had to wait for others to finish. They mixed
the custard and jelly to a pink pap and served it in
the same mugs, then poured a grey liquid that passed
for tea into the mugs sticky with soup, custard,
jelly and spittle.
```

I haven't eaten today. There is nothing in the fridge but a remnant of ox liver going black. Wrinkling my nose, I throw it away. In despair I survey the chaos of my daily life. Would Cynthia look after me, cook for me, keep my house in order? I'm a fool, but she protested her love.

'When I'm with you, I walk on a cloud.'

'Do you mean that?'

'Of course, darling, A wonderful, soft, fluffy cloud.'

She looked at me with those dark, melting eyes. She picked up the bill. It was astronomical: we had lobster thermidor and Bollinger '76 with Jack's money. We kissed in the taxi on the way back to Springfield, and she paid for the taxi. When we got there we made love on the white shagpile, still in our clothes.

A car swung into the drive. 'Quick, out the back.' I stood in the garden, zipping up my pants. I glanced through the window as I crept to the gate and saw the shoulder-length white hair.

'Christian, will you have a cup of tea?'

I ducked into the bushes as she turned to the window and drew the curtains.

The yard was a rectangle enclosed on three sides by brick walls and barred windows and, on the fourth, by a high corrugated-iron fence. A gazebo rose in the centre. Here the patients spent their days. Card players quarrelled and an old fellow with jerking limbs half-heartedly swept fallen leaves from one place to another with a worn broom. The bullring patients dozed in chairs under a canvas awning, about thirty of them, senile or burnt-out incontinent alcoholics.

McNaughton always complained about his head. 'Oh, my fractured skull, oh, my fractured skull.' His head was bald, smooth, round, pink. The charge attendant and Larry tiptoed up behind him and patted him on the head. McNaughton lamented louder. The louder he cried, the harder they slapped. 'Oh, my fractured skull, oh, my fractured skull.'

I want to see Cleaver grovel, to see the terror in his eyes. It's not enough to trigger a quick bolt into his heart on a dark night. I want him to know why he is getting his due, I want him to understand the depths of my hatred for him. I can respect Jack, Cleaver I can only loathe. Jack, after all, is Cynthia's husband. A husband is something you have to accept when you are involved with a married woman, an inconvenient fact of life, but another lover, no. Certainly not the Reverend Cleaver, Rasputin, the Man of God with the biblical quotation on his lips.

'"Love your enemies,"' he said, '"bless them that curse you."' He sat on one of Cynthia's velvet chairs, the tea cup between his thick fingers. 'The world,' he added, explaining why so much forgiveness is necessary, 'is full of bastards.' The antagonism between us was electric. Cynthia's dark eyes glittered: the spectacle of two males locking horns turned her on.

Not five minutes before, she and I had made love in this very room, on the rug. Then the car arrived and she shunted me out through the back door. When I saw that it was Cleaver, I walked boldly to the front door and rang the bell. I was damned if I was going to yield territory to Cleaver.

I think it was then that I first felt the desire to murder him. And I believe he feels the same way about me.

I'll kill him, even if they send me to prison or to the psychiatric ward.

At night, each patient received another mug of the grey tea and two slices of bread and butter. The bullring patients were taken inside, undressed and put to bed.

The others had to strip in the corridor, then wait, naked, outside their rooms while the attendants made the rounds, unlocking their doors, then locking them again behind them.

15

JONESY'S EGG-SHAPED HEAD drooped from his round shoulders, his wet lower lip dangled.

'Wanna cigarette, wanna cigarette...'

Larry rolled Jonesy a cigarette from dead leaves he had picked up in the yard. He ran his tongue along the edge, finished it neatly, gave it to Jonesy and offered him a light. Jonesy sucked at it greedily, reducing it to nothing in a series of rapid puffs, giving off clouds of black, pungent smoke like an incinerator.

I laughed.

'How did you like the cigarette?' Larry asked, grinning, when Jonesy had spat out the butt.

'Bloody awful, bloody awful.' Jonesy's eyes watered. 'Wanna proper cigarette, proper cigarette.'

Larry lit one for himself and blew its fragrance under Jonesy's quivering nose. 'I bet you do.' He changed the subject. 'Tell me, Jonesy, how often have you been in jail?'

'Twice, twice, twice,' Jonesy blabbered.

'Well, what do you know. What did you do?'

'Stole a pair o' cuff links, cuff links, cuff links.'

'What in Christ would you want cuff links for?'

'Sold 'em. Sold 'em. To buy grog.'

'I bet you did. What about the other time?'

'Stole a bicycle, bicycle.'

'Did you sell that too?'

'Yes, to buy grog, grog, grog.'

'Hasn't done you much good, has it?' Larry smirked wickedly. 'And how did you like it in jail? Or is it nicer here?'

'Leave me alone, you bastard, bastard.' Jonesy shuffled away, his greasy slippers flapping.

I laughed, but my laugh worried me.

I played chess with Dick Manley.

Manley, one of the privileged ones, was allowed to stay up after the others were locked in for the night. He sat in the day room, his pile of chess books at his elbow and one of his six or seven sets ready on the table. Chess was his passion, but he always lost. His skull was full of holes, and he wore a cyclist's headguard to protect himself when he fell down in one of his epileptic fits. As soon as the latest hole healed, they had him back in the operating theatre for more brain surgery, but he continued to have his fits. The headguard made him look like a second-rate boxer's stand-in sparring partner.

'I got sunstroke, you see, helping in the orchard, and that's what started it. Then they shoved me into hospitals and started to fuck around with my head. Look at my fuckin' head.' He tapped the headguard. 'Do you know how old I am? Twenty-six. And I've been in fuckin' hospitals since I was ten. I've never had a girl in my life.'

I let him win the game. We sipped hot tea. Manley's eyes rolled upwards and the rim of his cup rattled against his teeth. Hot tea slopped in all directions. I caught the cup. A brief, quivering, rolling convulsion, and he shook his head and blinked. He set up the men for another game. I didn't laugh.

It was hot, that Adelaide summer of 1959–60. It was to be my last summer in Australia for fifteen years. I had left school and my stepfather's house at sixteen and had been a failed printer's apprentice, fumbling service station attendant, incompetent cashier, and reluctant packer in the hardware department of a big store. Perhaps my best days in those dreary years were spent working as assistant projectionist for one of the cinema circuits: perched in the narrow bio-box by the whirring projector, tasting the sweet fumes and the heat of the arc lamp, peering through the porthole over the heads of the audience at the magic on the screen. But there was no future in it, and I left, working my way determinedly upward, to write radio jingles for a small advertising agency in Waymouth Street ('Dad, do you want your lawn as smooth as the top of a silk hat? Buy an Atco Roller Motor Mower . . .') When I could stomach that no more, I used my savings, all of two hundred pounds, to go back to school. I ended the year with my School Leaving Certificate, able to recite the whole of *Caesar*, and with five pounds left in the bank. The job at Parkside rescued my finances. I was able to save my fare back to Europe, third class by sea – eighty-seven pounds.

I was transferred to the imbecile ward. I waded through a knee-deep tangle of dirty sheets into deafening pandemonium and a stench of shit. Big Hanson, in charge, his sleeves rolled up, cleared a path through the melee with both elbows. 'You're just in time!' We dragged and kicked the imbeciles out of their beds – so close together that they had to crawl over each other – and herded them to the bathroom, caricature faces, gibbering, drooling, shit-smeared, dangling misshapen arms, hopping on twisted legs. We prodded them under the showers with mop handles, scrubbed them down with the mops, put overalls on them and stuck their feet into stinking tennis shoes from a mountain of stinking tennis shoes. Then we drove them to the dining room, where they gurgled and slobbered and dribbled, porridge flowing down their chins and their overalls, until the clock said eight and they were disgorged into the yard.

'And all this,' said Big Hanson, 'is my domain. Here, I'm ruler, emperor, king. My subjects love, respect and obey me, within their wretched limitations. Or they bloody well better, if they know what's good for them. I got 'em trained.'

He stuck two fingers in his mouth and whistled. A creature with grotesquely angled limbs and a narrow head shambled up crabwise. Hanson pointed at a Down's Syndrome boy who squatted, monkey-like, on the ground. The crab got down on all fours, pulled out the boy's penis and sucked.

'See?' Hanson looked like a lion tamer in a circus.

Thomas was different. His piss soaked his overalls, but he had a finely chiselled, sensitive face. I was drawn to him and asked his name. He said, 'Thomas' in a sad, cultured voice. I asked more questions and he answered them. He had a university degree, a wife and son. And now he stood here and wet himself. He intrigued me. If I could only find the key, a switch or trigger, I could jolt him out of his apathy.

'You can walk out of here. Pull yourself together. Tell yourself, Enough of this, I want to get on with my life,' I shouted at him. 'Don't you want to get out of here?'

He looked at me with his sad eyes. 'No,' he whispered. And stood there in his soiled overalls and his stinking tennis shoes.

'Would you kill them?'

Big Hanson, Dutch and I sat in the shade of a tree and discussed euthanasia.

'The main problem,' Hanson said, chewing gum, 'is responsibility. Who wants to take the responsibility?'

'They are people,' insisted Dutch, 'human beings, not animals.' Dutch prided himself on being a Christian. Short, round-faced, with owl-like spectacles, he looked after the 'babies', thirty imbecile children aged from two to twenty, crowded together in a small building at the back of K ward. They were dirty and needed constant watching, the worst job in the hospital.

'They're lower than animals,' Hanson said. 'Animals, at least, have all their faculties, or they wouldn't survive.'

Dutch shook his head. 'There is still a difference between people and animals.'

Hanson spat out his gum. 'Don't you believe it! I've worked in this place long enough to know. There isn't.'

'The Nazis gassed them,' I said.

'The Nazis killed normal people, too. We had the Nazis in Holland. Don't talk to me about the Nazis.'

'The main problem is responsibility,' repeated Hanson. 'Who's going to take the responsibility? They hanged the Nazis.'

We led the Soviet commissars into a room disguised as a doctor's surgery. They were told that they were to be given a medical examination. They were weighed and made to stand against a measuring rod fixed to the wall. There was a slot in the rod. A rifleman in a sound-proofed room on the other side of the wall fired through the slot, into the back of the prisoner's neck.

'It wasn't the killing that was the problem. It was disposing of the bodies . . .'

I'll leave Cleaver where he falls. I don't have the means to dispose of the body.

I know that I haven't the stomach to cut him up, the very thought makes me retch. And I probably couldn't move him: he weighs at least a hundred kilograms. It'd be like shifting a sack of stones. Perhaps I can lure him to some lonely place in the bush where he won't be found. He may come if he thinks it's about Cynthia. The summer sun has baked the ground as hard as fired clay. It'll be hard to bury the body. I'll have to cover him with sticks and leaves, and someone is bound to stumble on him, drawn by the smell and the flies. And I'll have to dispose of the car.

Only Cynthia links me to Cleaver. Will she connect me with his death? 'The world is full of bastards,' he said.

Perhaps the suspicion will fall on Jack.

'When you shot the commissars, were you acting under orders?'

'Yes.'

'When you kicked and beat the prisoners, when you drowned them in sewage, were you also acting under orders?'

'No.'

'Were you acting under orders when you hosed water down prisoner's throats until their bellies burst?'

'No.'

'Then why did you do it?'

'I don't know.'

'You don't know?'

'It wasn't permitted. We just did it. It was something that grew.'

Kicking Weston was something that grew. That morning when I entered the wards for the first time, I would never have imagined myself kicking Weston in the shins while Larry and the charge attendant laughed.

Having kicked Weston, I can kill Cleaver. Larry and the charge attendant are my mentors, my accomplices.

16

I'M IN THE SHELTER. The bombs sound like distant thunder, rolling closer. In the dim light, the faces are grey. Beside me sits a man in tall boots with a silver skull on his cap. My eyes return again and again to the skull. The face below the peak of the cap is as grey as the others, there is black stubble on his chin and he smells of stale sweat.

A boy plays with a toy Red Indian. The Red Indian has a feather head-dress and swings a tomahawk. I envy the boy, I want the Red Indian. My mother tells me that the boy's family was bombed out and all he has left is the Red Indian, but I still want it, I still envy the boy.

Another roll of thunder. I'm more afraid of the all-clear than of the bombs, because then we will have to go outside to the dust and the smoke and the smell of burning.

A motor car has been blown on to the roof of a block of flats and hangs there, a blue motor car, its front wheels over the gutter, its back broken. From a branch of a splintered tree dangles a human arm, the fingers grasping air, naked and strangely white but red raw where it was torn from the shoulder, like a joint in a butcher's shop.

'When the war is over, we'll go to Australia,' whispers my mother; 'we'll be with Grandpa and Grandma in their big house in Melbourne.' The promised land. I imagined Australia like the picture postcard I'd seen of a coral island: fronded palms against a round moon over a silvery sea. But, in Adelaide, I had to stand at attention while my Jewish stepfather reached out and hit me in the face with an iron hand.

I couldn't hit back. Not at the Flying Fortresses, nor at the Russian with the flame-spitting machine pistol, nor at the jeering youths hurling rocks outside the camp near Compiegne. I couldn't hit back at my stepfather. I rammed my anger and my hatred deep down in my guts.

But I could hit back at Israel Fish. We were in the same English class for immigrant children. He looked very Jewish. I can't remember why Fish and I were suddenly fighting in the playground, but I struck him again and again until the blood poured down his face. There was something immensely satisfying about hitting Fish, about his red flowing blood.

When I hammered Fish's semitic face, was I thrashing the hated Jew in myself?

'You should put the past behind you,' says Mupp. 'You can't go on feeding on your hatred forever.'

'I will put it behind me. There's just one thing I must do first.'

'You know what I think about that.'

'I have to do it.'

His glass eyes are round. 'Why?'

'You know why!'

'No, I don't. None of the reasons hold water.'

'All right, in self-defence. It's him or me. Because, if I don't get him first, he'll get me.'

'Do you really believe that?' Mupp shakes his head. 'You weren't always like this. You're using the past as an excuse. Others have suffered too. More than you.'

'Others! What do I care about others?'

'But you want them to care about you! You had everything, a wife, a child, a career. And you let them go. In exchange for what? Cynthia?'

Cynthia is not here. Cynthia has betrayed me.

Ingrid was there, for almost twenty years. She was always there, steady and dependable. It never occurred to me that she would leave one day. Perhaps I lost her because I was too certain of her.

They met in Hamburg, in the bookshop on the Stephansplatz. Her head was a mass of chestnut curls and her eyes were brown flecked with green. She was leafing through Hamsun's <u>Mysteries</u>. Their eyes met, they smiled, and on an impulse, he asked her to have coffee with him. They both had the day off and they spent the afternoon together, wandering in the gardens along the Alster.

I pause to read what I have written. How flat it seems. As so often now, I can't find the words to match the memory. For the first time in many months, Ingrid stands vividly before me, not as she is now but as she was then, when we were both young and life was ahead of us, and we were filled with hope and expectations. I can see the scene of our first meeting, alive in every detail. I can sense the mood. But the palette of my vocabulary has muddied, the canvas is smeared. I roll the sheet from the machine, but I do not tear it up. Instead I fold it down the middle, hiding the words, and slide it under the small sheaf of typed pages that is slowly building up.

On the bookshelves, I find the copy of *Mysteries*; she gave it to me. Between the pages there is a photograph of her taken when she was eighteen or twenty. She looks solemn, almost melancholy: the dark, straight brows under the strong forehead, the straight, classical nose, the serious eyes and mouth. The melancholy is accentuated by the setting. She is sitting on a straight chair in an attic room with a sloping wall, the small window behind her is overhung with vines. Her left hand rests in the lap of her full, dark skirt, the right fingers the beads of a triple-stranded necklace at her throat. I have always loved the curve of her throat and her soft small hands and tapered fingers.

On the flyleaf, in her large and rounded script, she has copied out a poem by Heinrich Heine. A premonition, a prophecy? She wrote it there on our wedding day:

> We felt much for each other, but we got on
> excellently all the same.
> We often played 'man and wife', but we didn't
> quarrel or fight. We rejoiced and laughed together
> and tenderly kissed and hugged.
> In the end, in childlike joy, we played hide
> and seek in the forests and fields,
> And hid so well,
> That we will never find each other again.

The sweat pearls on my arms.

The jackpump clunks and shrieks.

I shut it out.

I am in the bunker, where it is safe. The walls are made of concrete, metres thick. The concrete is green and you can see the woodgrain pattern of the boards between which it was poured.

The bombs rumble outside, but as long as I am in the bunker, I am safe. My mother is with me, and I know that the Fuehrer watches over us.

Bombs, more distant now. I do not want the bombs to stop; I want to stay in the bunker forever. When the bombs stop, the dreaded all-clear will sound and we will have to go out into the world of fire and death.

'When the war is over we'll go to Australia.' And I see the scene from the picture postcard, the fronded palms, the moon, the silver sea.

There are no fronded palms here, just bush and paddock, the paddocks parched, burnt yellow. I draw the blinds and curtains, run water into the handbasin and splash my face and neck. The tap spits, coughs and expires. The damned power has failed again. I try the light switch, the lights are working; perhaps the pressure system has broken down? I wind a towel around myself, find my glasses, pull on my shoes and stumble outside. My knuckles rap the corrugated-iron tank and it resounds, booming, empty. Two days ago the water still stood two feet above the outlet; enough, if used sparingly, to last until the rain. I check the pipes and the pump, then see the hole in the tank, a few inches from the bottom, small and round and jagged inwards, a bullet hole, probably from a .22 rifle.

I wonder where the shot came from? Was it from the rise behind the house that is covered in dense scrub? Who would want to hole my tank? Some trigger-happy yob, one of the so-called sportsmen from the suburbs who make the countryside unsafe on weekends by potting at road signs, silos, cattle, water tanks? I have a second tank that collects the rainwater from the shed. To my relief it is undamaged and almost full, but this one isn't connected to the house and I'll have to fetch my water in a bucket until I can plug and refill the main tank.

Back in the house my sense of anger and dread has heightened. A stray bullet, some irresponsible yob? Or has someone got it in for me? From the drawer I take the flintlock, which I haven't touched since I almost killed myself. Rust is forming in the barrel and in the touch hole. I clean and oil and load the gun and put it before me on the table, beside the crossbow, four bolts ready, pointed, deadly.

Insects hum electrically, spiralling into the night light, their bodies beating against the screens like many tapping fingers. The crickets rattle like tiny pneumatic drills, a cacophony that almost drowns out the clunk and shriek. Ingrid and I sat here on hot summer nights and watched the frenzy of the moths under the verandah light.

My need for a woman burns in my gut. Fantasies of Ingrid, of Cynthia, they become one.

Four letters are still unanswered. There are Phyllis, the widow with the two teenage sons; Dianne, the divorcee who plays ten-pin bowls; Cathy, the telephonist into Chinese cooking; and the other Carol, the full-time student, who is separated and has three growing daughters.

I decide I'll try Cathy. Perhaps she'll invite me to one of her Chinese meals. And her letter didn't mention children.

'Hello?' The voice is feminine, melodious.

I clear my throat. 'Is that Cathy? I'm the author. I had an ad in the paper. I received your reply.'

An awkward pause. 'I've met someone. But thank you for calling.'

She has hung up. My vision of Chinese dishes followed by romantic delights collapses. I'm a fool. I should have called her before. I liked her voice. I decide to ring Dianne. There are worse pursuits than ten-pin bowls.

'Dianne here.' Irritable, broad strine. 'Who is it?'

'I'm the author. I had an ad in the paper. You replied.'

'What ad? Oh, that was ages ago. You're calling late. I was in bed.'

'I'm sorry...'

'Where are you from. I wanted an Australian.' She pronounces it 'Orstrailian'.

'I'm naturalised.'

'I mean, a born Australian. I had a bad experince with someone from another race.'

Can she sense the Jew in me? 'I'm not yellow, or black. Maybe we can meet for coffee and talk.'

'No, I want an Australian. I don't think you'd be right.'

'If that's how you feel.'

'You wouldn't be right.'

Stupid woman! That leaves Phyllis and the second Carol. Two teenage sons, three growing daughters. Anyway, it's after

ten, too late to call them now. I'm tense and angrier than before.
The moths beat a tattoo against the screens, the crickets go
rattat-rattat. From his chair by the door the Reverend Christian
Cleaver gives me a malevolent look.

The heat, the insects, the jackpump, the night. A bullet in
my tank. Is someone out there? I strain my ears. The flintlock
cocked in my hand, I peer into the dark.

17

They lived on the Haake, a forest that had stood
since the beginning of time, and they knew every track
and trail and every tree, the slim pale beeches and the
dark towering pines. In summer, tiny flies buzzed in the
sunny clearings. In autumn, the paths were carpets of
golden leaves and winter covered everything in
glistening white. In spring, the sunbeams reached down
again, and Ingrid took off her clothes and ran naked
through the woods.

I MUST ORDER the fragments and finish my reconstruction
of The Book. But my mind is in chaos, The Book a ragged
pile of bits and pieces, without a beginning or an end. And
Cleaver preys on me, the meaty face comes between me and the
paper, the trumpeting voice fills my ears and drowns out every
other thought.

Rasputin knows that I am planning to kill him, knows
because he has decided to murder me, decided my death long
ago, long before that first homicidal impulse entered my mind.
'The world is full of bastards,' he said as we sat on Cynthia's
gold velvet chairs, facing each other like fighting cocks across

the white shagpile on which she and I had made love only minutes before. ' "Love your enemies," ' he said. ' "Bless them that curse you." ' But I knew what he was thinking; there was murder in his voice and his eyes. And that is why I have to kill him: I must get him before he gets me. The bullet in the tank was a warning. Of course the bullet was fired by Cleaver; he is stalking me, is probably out there now, hiding in the scrub with his rifle, a silenced sniper rifle with a telescopic sight; he is watching my door, my windows. I'm a sitting duck: the moment I leave the house I'm out in the open. And he is in cover, sitting pretty, with his rifle at the ready and a six-pack in his esky, waiting in the shade.

He has all the time in the world because my throat is parched, I have run out of water, and the bucket is empty. I need a drink, but I can't go out to refill the bucket because he will get me. That was his plan: hole the tank to force me out of the house, then shoot me down in cold blood. Well, he has miscalculated; he is not going to get me. I can do without water, I can do without food. I can do without water until tonight. I will fetch my water in the dark when I have the advantage because he can't use his telescopic sight, and I know the ground. Then I'll stalk him; the little crossbow with four bolts in the barrel is handier in the dark than his rifle, and it is silent.

I must not show any lights, that's all, so that my shadow won't fall on the blinds. As soon as it is dark, my turn will come, and it will be the end of Cleaver.

The end of Rasputin.

'You're mad,' says Cleaver. At first I thought it was Mupp who spoke, but it was Cleaver. There is hatred on the paperbag face. Hatred and fear; he has every reason to fear me. 'You're mad,' he repeats, and his voice is strangled, but he is alive. My hatred has given him life as my love once gave life to Mupp. But what I have given I can take away. I aim the crossbow and send four quick bolts into his red paper heart.

'You are mad,' cackles Cleaver. 'You are mad,' cries Mupp. 'Mad, mad, mad,' they shout in chorus, and I cover my ears.

I need water, but I must wait until tonight when it is dark. If Cleaver has a nightsight on his rifle, he'll be able to pick me out in the dark as clearly as if it were day.

The bulldozers moved in before dawn on a day that caught the protesters unaware. And for months, there was only the scream of the chainsaws and the roar of the diesels. The work ended, but the peace of the forest was shattered. Cars poured along concrete where Ingrid once danced naked in the sunbeams that fell through the leaves.

Let Cleaver kill me, let him do his worst. I don't care. I'll walk out there, unprotected, I almost welcome the end, the swift bullet that will strike me down.

Bucket in hand, I step out of the back door. My chest is bare. Now he has me in his sights. How many seconds of life are left? I wonder when the deadly bullet will come.

I advance into the bright sunlight. Now I am out in the open, where there is no cover. Surely he has seen me by now. I steel myself for the bullet that will tear through my shoulder or smash my jaw.

I halt. What is he waiting for?

'Cleaver!' I shout.

'Cleaver! Cleaver!'

'Damn you! Here I am!' I point at my chest. 'Damn you, shoot!'

'Shoot, you bastard, shoot!'

He is playing games. He wants me to think that I am safe, then shoot me when I am not expecting it. I walk to the tank, stoop and fill the bucket from the tap, my muscles tensed against the bullet that will strike me between the shoulder blades. I walk back to the house.

I have reached the door. Each step has taken an eternity. I am inside. He hasn't fired. I put down the bucket. I am trembling, my knees are weak.

Why hasn't he fired? I know that he is out there, up on the hill, in the bush waiting.

He hasn't fired because he wants to prolong my terror before he shoots me dead.

I am trapped in the house by that vengeful madman with the rifle. The house is a choking oven; the sweat pours in rivers down my body and wets everything I touch; only my mouth is dry. I scoop water from the bucket, sip, then pour it back. I must discipline myself; I must make the water last. Cautiously, I raise one corner of a blind. Where is he? I must keep away from the windows. The blinds are down and the curtains closed, but the windows are vulnerable, an obvious target. He may take a potshot at a window in the hope of hitting me by chance or of injuring me with flying glass, a shard in my jugular or in my eye. The whole house is vulnerable – the walls are no protection, a bullet would punch straight through the fibro-cement sheets, and he must know it; he could shoot up the house, riddle it like a sieve, and nobody would hear the shots. But he is in no hurry, if he had wanted to kill me quickly he could have dropped me without warning when I stepped outside. What I can't do is to call for help. I can't call the police. This is between me and Cleaver, for the two of us to settle. And only one will survive the final showdown, him or me.

On the wall the little pendulum clock with the hand-painted face ticks nervously, tick-tack, tick-tack: it's the clock Ingrid left behind. Five past five. Four more hours until dark; we are on summer time, an extra hour of daylight. Tick-tack, tick-tack. Four more hours.

Are you enjoying yourself, Cleaver? It is hot out there under the naked sun. Is your hand steady, are you comfortable in the dust and the prickly scrub? Or are the ants climbing up your pants? Are the flies buzzing you? Is the sun scorching your pink, tender neck? You do know that I know that you're out there, don't you, Cleaver? That was part of your plan, that I should know.

Don't take my silence for cowardice, Cleaver; don't think I'm shitting myself because you're out there with a gun. Let's brighten this up a little, some music to help the time pass? I start the tape and turn the sound up full. The throaty voices of the stormtroopers, loud enough to lift the roof.

Die Fahne hoch! Die Reihen fest geschlossen!

I join in, bawling at the top of my lungs.

SA marschiert mit ruhig festem Schritt...

Do you hear that, Cleaver, up there, on the hill?

Cleaver, I defy you! The Flag Flies On! We must not show cowardice to a mocking world but raise the old swastika banner in wild and fanatical resistance! I'm coming to get you, Cleaver, I'm coming out!

Stark naked, the crossbow in one hand, the flintlock in the other, I leap outside and race across the open ground and up the hill. Behind me the Brownshirts thunder. I shout their song.

Die Strasse frei den braunen Bataillonen!

Clear the road for the brown battalions!

Hurrah! Hurrah!

Charge!

I have reached the crest and still no bullet. Fight, you swine! Something moves, I point the pistol, the flint strikes sparks, the gun goes off with a boomph and a cloud of smoke. I crash through the scrub into the clearing. No sign of him. Damn you, coward! He has lost his nerve and fled.

I recover my breath. Something gleams in the hot sand. I pick it up. A .22 cartridge case. Cleaver was here all right. I have the proof.

I clean, oil and reload the gun; I must be prepared. Before me on the table stands the cartridge case, a small brass cylinder.

It's too hot to sleep. My skin burns, I'm scratched all over from my naked charge through the bush, and my feet are cut. The bucket is empty again, but I can't fix the tank while Cleaver lurks about.

18

'YOU KNOW that Cleaver isn't trying to kill you.' Mupp's round glass eyes are fixed on me.

'You were here,' I snap.

The round eyes are unblinking. 'I saw no Cleaver.'

'You would be dead now if I hadn't attacked, if he hadn't lost his nerve. You know that if he kills me, you're dead too. I'm the one who gives you life.'

'Don't remind me.'

'I charged and he ran.'

'All I saw was you, puffing up the hill like a maniac.'

I must convince him. 'The cartridge case.'

'That could have been dropped by anyone.'

'It was fired by Cleaver. Who else would want to kill me?'

'Nobody wants to kill you.'

'The hole in the tank. That's all in my mind, too?'

'A stray shot. Or some yob. You thought so yourself.'

'Cleaver.'

'You're making it up, like your stories. You're losing the distinction between fact and fantasy.'

Mupp's right. It wasn't Cleaver. Cleaver wasn't up the hill. Cleaver isn't trying to kill me. I'm telling myself that Cleaver is trying to kill me to justify my desire to murder him. I'll put Cleaver out of my mind. I'll spend the rest of the afternoon writing. There was a time when I spent hours at my old Remington, when the thoughts flowed, when I regularly produced five thousand words a day.

I fling open the curtains and snap up the blinds. Sunlight streams in. I uncover the typewriter. My fingers toy with the keys. Once I have the first sentence the rest will flow. I chew my fingers, which are covered with calluses from chewing, pace the room and step to the window. The yellow hills stretch before me under the vast blue sky. A movement in the valley catches my eye. A distant figure: he stands on the road and looks up at my house. His hat brim shades the upper part of his face; do I see a flash of white, a white beard? I snatch the binoculars from the bookcase, my hands shaking, and a yellow blur dances before my eyes. I twist the focus wheel and scan the road. He is gone. A cloud of brown dust drifts away, the sound of a departing car.

No question of writing now. I must protect myself! I need a guard dog – a German Shepherd or a Dobermann – heavy and vicious enough to maul an intruder. I should have bought a guard dog long ago. But Cleaver wouldn't let a dog stop him, he'd shoot or poison it. I remember the old barbed wire left when I replaced the fences after the fires. If I can stop him from getting on the hill behind the house, I'll have robbed him of his advantage; it's from the hill that he commands a clear field of fire. I'll throw up a barricade, barbed-wire entanglements. He won't dare climb the hill in daylight, and at night the wire will trap him. Where are my shorts, my boots? I scramble down the slope. The wire is there, great rusted rolls shot through with grass. It takes all my strength to lever the rolls free of the grass. The rusted wire is stiff and brittle, and a barb reopens the gash in my forearm; the sun blazes down. I ignore the blood that trickles, thickly, down my arm and into my glove. I rest, then drag the wire up the hill.

Flushed and exhausted, I return to the house. The wire isn't enough: I'll devise some booby traps, pointed stakes in the ground and tripwires, an alarm system using string and tin cans. But even then I won't be safe, I won't be safe so long as Cleaver is alive.

I put my tape in the deck and carry the phone to the

speaker. 'May I speak to the Reverend Cleaver?' The quavering falsetto, Mrs Cecilia Beazley.

'He's still away. Can I give him a message?'

I hang up. If it was Cleaver I saw, where is he now?

My neck and shoulders burn lobster red – I was a fool to slave in the sun without hat or shirt – and the cut in my arm, which I swab with disinfectant, is deep and ugly. I can't remember when I had my last tetanus shot. Dirty dishes are piling up, I can't flush the lavatory and I need to fix the tank.

The typewriter stares at me accusingly. I walk up and down, trapped like the mangy wolf in his tiny cage in the travelling zoo that came with the carnival that set up its tents and stalls on the Heiligengeistfeld in Hamburg twice a year. Like an automatic slide projector gone mad, images flash inside my skull; somebody has jumbled the slides. Cleaver. Cynthia. Adolf Hitler. Larry and the charge attendant, their faces twisted in sadistic glee. The ten shabby men in the dock. The muzzle flashes of the Soviet submachine gun, a motor car on a roof, an arm in a tree. Ingrid naked in the wood. Khrushchev: chubby, pink, gleaming, polished with Mr Sheen. The blood, bright and satisfying, that poured down Israel Fish's semitic face while I pounded him, pounded the ugly little Jew in him, in me.

From the shelf, I pull *Mein Kampf*, the leather-bound, leaf fiftieth birthday edition, signed by the Fuehrer:

Obstacles are there not for us to capitulate to them, but to break them.

National Socialist willpower and discipline. They helped me survive my stepfather's punishing hand. I stood, rigid, chin up, chest out, belly in, shoulders square, my heels riveted together and my arms at my sides, while he reached out and smashed me in the face. I thought of the brave German soldiers at Stalingrad and did not give him the satisfaction of a flinch or a whimper.

'You don't really need me. You like the thought that I'm available, there at your beck and call. But you don't really need

93

me, my presence, my touch, my being with you.'

Cynthia's dark eyes were liquid, her soft hand was on my thigh. 'I do need you. You know I do.'

'Then show me. I want the proof. When you were sick, I came and cooked for you. Where were you when I was sick?'

She had no answer to that. She was in Surfers Paradise with Cleaver.

I shouldn't have let Ingrid go. I wallow in self-pity. I disgust me.

'Ingrid,' I cry.

The answer is a mocking silence.

'Helga!'

KEEP OUT! GENIUS AT WORK! The sign is still on the door of Helga's room. I turn the handle. I haven't used the room since they left. The elephants are still on the wallpaper, but Helga's bed and chest of drawers are gone; pale patches on the floorboards where they stood. Her little table and chair remain, outgrown. She has cut her intitials into the table top. Once I smacked her bottom for carving notches into the window sill. I run my fingers over the scars and I get grey dust on my fingertips.

Helga, your mother has kept you away from me. Do you remember when I cleared your blocked little nose and you smiled up at me from your cot and said, 'Haboo'? Or that mad ride in the ambulance when you swallowed all the fluoride tablets? Your busy little fingers managed to unscrew the lid, and I found you popping all the lovely little pink, yellow and green lollies into your mouth. Or before you were born, when I placed the zither against your mother's belly and gently strummed the strings and you kicked?

Ingrid wanted a home birth; she did all the right exercises but you refused to come. You grew bigger and bigger and Ingrid grew bigger with you. You were two weeks overdue, and then three. They had to get you out by Caesarian section. Ingrid felt cheated. I stood at the window in the sterile hospital corridor and a nurse held up a big pale baby with solemn blue-grey eyes; I had always thought new babies were red. It was our last

Christmas in Hamburg, and I bought Zimtsterne and Spekulatius.

'I always knew that one day I would go to Australia.' Ingrid's eyes, brown flecked with green, looked into the distance. 'In my teens, I read a novel by Arthur Upfield. It was about an old lady who lived in a hotel in Adelaide. I saw myself as an old lady in a hotel in Adelaide. And now we're really going there.

'It seemed fated, that we should meet in that bookshop,' she said, 'that you came from Adelaide.'

Yes, I am nothing more than a pawn of fate, my sole purpose to enter Ingrid's life so that one day she'll fulfill her destiny and be an old lady in a hotel in Adelaide. But I didn't know what awaited us as we packed. I had that vision of Australia as the Promised Land. This time, I was determined that I would not be beaten. I would find the picture postcard idyll that my mother had promised me as we huddled in the bunker.

My foot flat on the accelerator, I hurl the car into the curves. I race down the freeway past Eagle On The Hill and around Devil's Elbow. I slow at the traffic lights at Glen Osmond. Fifteen minutes later I stand outside the block of home units on Anzac Highway.

'Helga!' I shout up at the window. 'Helga!'

The window opens. Ingrid's head appears. 'I've asked you not to come here. It upsets me. It upsets her.'

'She's my daughter!'

'Not any more!' The window bangs shut and the blind comes down.

'Helga!' I shout hoarsely. Behind me, on Anzac Highway, the peak hour traffic roars.

I duck into the hall, pound up the stairs and hammer on the door. 'Helga!'

'Daddy . . .'

Ingrid says, 'Go away. I have a restraining order. Go away or I'll call the police.'

'Damn it, I want to see my child.'

The door across the hall opens and old Mrs Linden stares at me indignantly.

Defeated, I retreat to the car.

I turn the car towards Fullarton. Main South Road and Cross Road are one big traffic jam. I fume and sweat. Launder Avenue. I park around the corner, creep up the lane and peer over the fence. Cleaver's car is not in the carport. My next stop is Springfield.

Jack stands on the lawn in his shirtsleeves, garden hose in hand, sprinkling the rose bushes. I speed away.

The blood-red sun is sinking behind the hill when I return, and shadows are filling the valley. I tense as I leave the car to unlock the gate and scan the gloom. I drive in and replace the chain and padlock; I have stretched barbed wire along the top of the gate. The house is undisturbed; the typewriter stands uncovered and beside it sits Mupp, looking at me with his round glass eyes. The effigy of Cleaver, a bolt in the exposed heart, slumps in the chair by the door. I take the torch and the flintlock and slide outside again, the pistol in my right, the torch, switched off, in my left, and pad silently up the hill. I reach the wire. 'HAH!' I click on the torch and stab its beam into the bushes. Nobody.

19

'DON'T YOU abandon me. You're all I have left. There's no one else. No one.'

No answer.

'I need you.'

He remains silent.

'Stop playing games with me! Say something!'

His round glass eyes are impenetrable. I know that he's convinced that I'm crazy.

'You'll go into the Goodwill Box,' I shriek. 'Better still, I'll sell you. Old teddy bears are in demand. An American collector recently paid six thousand dollars for an eighty-year-old Steiff bear. You're a Steiff bear.'

'I'm only fifty.'

My threats have got through to him.

'Besides, I'm too shabby. Look at me. You wore off most of my fur.'

'That bear was shabby too.'

'Sell me then. At least I'll be appreciated.'

'You'll finish up in a glass case with a lot of other shabby bears.'

'That's better than ending up in a lunatic asylum with you. If a bushfire doesn't get us first.'

Cleaver smirks maliciously from his chair by the door.

'You keep out of this,' I snarl. 'You'll get yours.'

'Why don't you write your book,' says Mupp, 'and stop picking on us?'

'Us? Since when are you and Cleaver us?' They are ganging up on me.

He realises that he has gone too far.

'The world is still waiting for your book, remember? The book about the charge attendant and Larry, and Adolf Hitler, Sir John William Whitcombe, and me. Who was Sir John William Whitcombe, anyway?'

He was a little drunk who finished up in Parkside. He was only four feet high. He made up in nastiness what he lacked in height. 'You call me Sir, you bastards,' he yelled, stamping his foot. 'I am Sir John William Whitcombe, owner of the Kingston Arms Hotel.' Larry boxed his ears. 'You are Sir John William Arsehole and you swept the floor at the Kingston Arms Hotel.' 'Orright, orright,' Whitcombe muttered, 'I didn't say nuttin' anyway.' Whitcombe squeezed his shit through the peephole at night. He turned on all the taps in the bathroom and pushed the toilet rolls down the toilets, blocking the pipes.

Larry said that sobriety had been Whitcombe's downfall. On a dead, cold sober morning after a night in the cells, Whitcombe groped his way into the street, bang into the path of a truck, a beer delivery truck to boot. Anyone who knew Whitcombe in his prime, sweeping the floor and wiping the toilets at the Kingston Arms, who remembered how each pint and each quart of an interminable succession of pints and quarts added another inch to his stature, another grade to his status, made him more human, everybody's brother, would have agreed: only a cold sober Whitcombe would have groped his way into the path of a truck...

'I don't think I want to be in the same book as Whitcombe.' Mupp wrinkles his balding nose.

There are some who are condemned to walk endlessly along an interminable street of closed doors and blank walls. They put one foot ahead of the other and one foot ahead of the other and the blank walls and the closed doors move past. Others only have to approach a door and it is thrown open. Others knock, the door swings back, and they step inside. Others go from door to door, pounding and pleading, until at last a bolt is drawn and they slip through. But for a few, no doors open and they do not knock. They walk, putting one foot

ahead of the other, and the blank walls and the doors,
which may as well be blank walls, swim past. They walk
and walk, and their soles scrape the hard pavement as
their feet become heavy, and they carry the burden of
their bodies, the leaden vacuum inside them, down the
interminable street.

I find a scrap of paper, yellowed, the edges eaten jagged by
silverfish. When did I write that? On my first typewriter, in that
narrow room in Robsart Street, the size of a Parkside cell, just
big enough for the bed, a wardrobe, a table and a chair.

'I should write a book,' I tell Mupp, 'called *Bedsitters I Have
Known.*' From the age of sixteen, I lived in rented rooms. I was
to spend years in rented rooms sharing the use of the kitchen,
toilet and bath. They had threadbare carpets and ragged blinds,
were full of junk furniture, had lumpy mattresses on sagging
beds, ramshackle wardrobes with one bent wire hanger forlorn
on the rail, greasy armchairs with the springs poking through
the upholstery and the stuffing hanging out. In rented rooms
you are never private, never alone. There are banging doors,
footsteps in the hallway, coughing, laughter, muffled voices, a
constant medley of other people's radios, record players, TVs.
Penny-in-the-slot gas meters and queuing for the bathroom and
the kitchen stove. Strange room neighbours and stranger
landlords with petty rules and regulations – no visitors of the
opposite sex, no flushing the loo after 10 pm – who went
through your drawers and your dirty linen while you were out.

'I was in a suitcase,' says Mupp in a huff. 'You left me in a
stuffy old suitcase in your stepfather's garage.'

'You wouldn't have liked the room in Robsart Street. The
man in the next room snored. He was a big man who came
home from work at three in the morning and walked up and
down in heavy boots. When at last he went to sleep, his snoring
shook the wall. I had never heard anyone snore like that before.
I bought a bicycle horn, a cheap chrome-plated one with a red
rubber bulb. When the snoring started I put the horn to the wall

and honked. The snores would be interrupted by a splutter and his bedsprings creaked as he turned to the other side. If I was lucky, he stopped long enough for me to get back to sleep.

'One night I was awakened by a shuddering, creaking and crashing . . . It was worse than the 1954 earthquake. I staggered outside. There was a big tear in his blind. Through the hole, I could see the bed. A woman's legs were stuck out at an angle and between them was his huge arse, in violent motion. The woman had a blue sock on one of her feet. I returned to my room. Abruptly, the noise stopped. My curiosity drew me back outside. He had lit a cigarette and was giving her money. She looked down at herself and said, "Christ, I stink." '

'You revel in the sleazy side of life,' Mupp disapproves.

Wally, my landlord in Tooting in London, could levitate tables – a few passes of his hands, and the table would rise six feet off the floor. I never witnessed this miracle. Wally said that I was not spiritual enough; my presence interfered with his powers. He was a grey little man with alert brown eyes in a monkey face, and he had two Capuchin monkeys that roamed the house. The monkeys leapt on my shoulders and kissed me, poking at me with leathery little tongues.

On some malicious impulse, one darted its finger into my ear. Its finger was like a matchstick, with a sharp, pointed nail. I thought that my eardrum had been pierced. I had to get to the office, a forty-minute ride on the underground nursing my ear. A company doctor was on duty in the Reuter building on Fleet Street. He sat behind his desk. A medical student occupied a chair.

'What can I do for you?' the doctor asked.

'A monkey stuck its finger in my ear.'

The doctor looked at me solemnly. His mouth fell open and he gulped for air. He turned to the medical student, guffawed, hee-hawed. Beside himself, he shrieked, 'Did you hear that? A monkey stuck its finger in his ear!'

The medical student guffawed and shrieked.

'A monkey stuck its finger in his ear!'

The eardrum proved undamaged, and I left after I'd had a tetanus shot.

I reported at the newsdesk ten minutes late. 'A monkey stuck its finger into my ear' I said.

They looked at me solemnly. Then their mouths fell open. They guffawed, hee-hawed, shrieked.

'They were cruel,' says Mupp.

I defend them. 'It was really very funny.'

Before my shift ended, Kennedy was dead. The first flash came from United Press: KENNEDY SHOT. We waited, our systems pumping adrenalin. For minutes the constant chatter of the teleprinters seemed to have been interrupted. The newsroom was unnaturally silent; it was as if the world was holding its breath. I began to update the obituary that we kept on him as we did on all important people on file.

FLASH FLASH FLASH
KENNEDY DEAD

Within half an hour the first extras were in the street. I looked from the window; it was night and the newspaper offices along Fleet Street were, as always, brightly lit. The cries of the paperboys rose from below. People snatched the papers and stood stunned. By now the Reuter newsroom had moved into top gear: paper poured from the teleprinters, and every typewriter was hammering. After my shift ended at midnight I would join the late travellers on the tube. They looked numbed, as if war had been declared. Back in my upstairs room in the old terrace house on Tooting Bec Common I couldn't sleep and listened to the radio until dawn, heard Johnson sworn in as new President. I remembered Kennedy in Vienna, in Khrushchev's shadow.

I thrived on crises, I was charged as if by an electric current. Kennedy's death made me feel more alive.

I clear the workbench of rubbish, dust, cinders that drifted in after the fires, cobwebs. My tools, once lovingly cared for, rust on the racks, and there are tins of dried-up paint on the shelves, useless brushes, hard as rock. When Ingrid was here I spent the days measuring, sawing, planing, joining. We built and planted. The rabbits ate the trees and we planted more. We protected them with chicken wire and watered them by hand from buckets through the hot summer months. The first fire killed them all and we replanted. When the second fire came, the new blue gums were eight to ten feet high, too young to survive. The blackened trunks still stand, sticklike. The house, untouched by the flames, is unfinished, the door and window frames and fascias unpainted, the timber rotted by the rain and warped by the sun. Building material lies about. Ingrid is gone.

I find scraps of sheet iron, wire, nylon line, wooden pegs. I free the tinsnips with penetrating oil and cut out triangular pieces of iron. I will string them through the bush in the hope that their clatter will alert me when Cleaver comes. It is hard work, the snips blister my sweaty fingers, the sharp iron cuts my hands. The bandage on my arm is bloody. I throw iron and wire and pegs and line into the wheelbarrow, put the sledge hammer on top, and manoeuvre the barrow down the hill. A brown snake slithers away into the tall grass.

Below two inches of dust the ground is like iron, the pegs splinter under the hammer. Tiny black flies divebomb my eyes. This is childish. If Cleaver wants to get me he will get me. I abandon the wheelbarrow and stump back up the hill. All my efforts are doomed to failure.

'You fool,' Cleaver taunts me.

'Laugh at me. We'll see who has the last laugh.'

'Do you think Cynthia will come back to you?'

'You alienated her from me. You came between us.'

'If she really loved you, why would she turn to me?'

'You are her Rasputin. You have her in your power.'

'You overestimate me.'

'With you gone it will be like it used to be.'

'You've lost her. Do you know why?'

'Why?'

'She finished with you the moment Ingrid left you. The moment you were free, you became a threat.'

'Liar!' I clamp my hands over my ears, but I can still hear his mocking laughter.

20

I THRESH in my sweat on the rumpled sheet. The night squats on my gasping chest, choking me. If I survive the night Cleaver will kill me, unless I get him first.

The jackpump clunks and shrieks.

Is Cleaver out there in the night?

'Ingrid!' I reach out, but Ingrid isn't there.

Curse Cynthia. If it wasn't for Cynthia, Ingrid might still be here.

'Damn it, she's a friend, that's all. A good friend.' The blood shot to my head, fired by guilt. 'We all need friends.'

Ingrid persisted. 'I heard you speak to her on the phone. You spoke to her in the same voice in which you used to speak to me.'

'If you mean, are Cynthia and I having an affair, the answer is no!' I ran out of the house, slamming the door so that the windows rattled.

Ingrid and I were on separate islands then. Since her father died, a wall had gone up around her that I could not penetrate, and I fled to Cynthia.

'How alike we are.' Cynthia's small, warm hand touched mine. 'Look at our hands. They have the same shape. We are clones, you and me.'

'Will you divorce Jack?'

'My marriage to Jack is dead. There's nothing left. I tried. I tried for years. But he moves in another world, a world I'm not part of.'

'Will you divorce him?'

She was silent.

'Will you?'

'I'll see my solicitor. There are lots of things to be sorted out. Jack can be utterly ruthless.'

But I knew that she was afraid to lose her Lamborghini and the Springfield home with ducted air-conditioning and heated indoor pool. That I could never fulfil her demands.

And there is Cleaver.

Her hand was on my thigh. 'Come to bed.'

I writhe on the bed, alone, while the pump clunks and shrieks, and curse Cynthia, who would destroy me. I scream my curses into the night.

My time is running out. Everything is moving towards a resolution, the inevitable explosion, a violent and bloody climax. And The Book, my testament, is still a pitiful pile of scattered notes. I beat my brow with my fist. I want to leave The Book for Helga, so that one day she will understand.

I will finish The Book in prison or in the psychiatric ward if I survive. Some of the greatest books were written in prison. *In the Belly of the Beast. Notre-Dame-des-fleurs. One Hundred and Twenty Days of Sodom.*

Mein Kampf.

'There is one word that I have never learned, and that is capitulation...'

The rasping voice, charged with raw sexuality. The Demon, I cannot get rid of him. I wonder if Helga will ever understand, Helga, who has my mother's Jewish face.

I stumble at my mother's side through the smoke and the rubble. The remains of a piano, a tangle of wires, the singed ivories grinning like stained teeth. Houses laid open, their fronts gone, opened like you can open a doll's house, the furniture undisturbed, beds, wardrobes, chairs arranged around a dining table, pictures on the walls.

A picture of Hitler.

My mother pulls me by the hand. She is carrying my brother. I carry Mupp.

Slogans on broken walls in big white letters. KAMPF BIS ZUM SIEG. Fight on to victory. WIR DANKEN UNSEREM FUEHRER. We thank our leader.

Between raids, we boys searched for bomb and shell fragments, torn and twisted pieces of steel, aluminium and brass. My prize was the casing of a British thermite bomb, octagonal, hollow, more than a foot long. Looking for shrapnel trained my eyes. If there's a cent in the gutter, I'll find it.

In Australia, we saluted the flag and marched into school to drums and fifes. I joined the scouts and the school cadets; instead of Hitler there was the King and Baden-Powell. The father figure of Bob Menzies, with the bushy black eyebrows, the silver hair and the booming voice, British to the bootstraps, protected us from Godless Communism and preserved our Democratic Way of Life. Australia was a Free Country in the Free World. We were on the Side of Right; the future stretched before us, golden as a *Reader's Digest* scenario: The Power of Prayer. Cancer Can Be Cured. The Atom: Hope of Mankind. There was the Yellow Peril, of course, but without a peril, how do you know that you're on the Side of Right?

Helga is convinced that she won't grow up to be an adult, that we'll all be nuked, or pollute ourselves to death, or die of AIDS.

Today the young have nothing to believe in. Bring back Bob Menzies; bring back the drums, the fifes and the flag. Bring back Biggles and Captain Marvel. Bring back the radio thrillers, *Dossier on Demetrius, Forty-Eight Hours.* Bring back the Saturday matinees; the cinema filled with the sweet smell of bubble gum and the screaming of the kids, admission one shilling, *Hopalong Cassidy* and *Tarzan*, cartoons and the serials, each chapter ending on a cliffhanger, the hero fighting for his life on top of a runaway stagecoach, the girl trapped in a cage with a roaring gorilla. 'Will she escape? See the next thrilling chapter at this theatre next week!' The horror shows at the old Mayfair in Rundle Street! My stepfather strictly forbade me to see *Frankenstein*. For weeks afterwards I imitated Boris Karloff, stepping slowly with a stiff, heavy gait, my arms hanging loosely at my sides, fingers extended like claws, staring glassily, the corners of my mouth pulled down, a little scared of myself.

'You hated Adelaide in the fifties,' jeers Mupp. 'That's why you went back to Europe.'

'I hated my stepfather, the illiterate, chip-on-the-shoulder small-town Jew from Slovakia. I hated having to leave school when all my friends went on to university. I hated the rented rooms, I hated my jobs, and I hated the wowserism, the censorship, the banning of books...'

'But you yearn for Menzies.'

'Mere nostalgia. I saw Menzies speak at the Adelaide Town Hall. He stood there, big under the lights. "I won't have a bar of it," he thundered and he looked straight at me from below those black brows. I think he was talking about communism. "I won't have a bar of it." I was impressed.'

'You do yearn for Menzies. And the drums, the fifes and the flag. Like you yearn for Hitler.'

'I yearn for structure. For order, security.'

'Order for everybody else, but not for yourself.'

'I've discovered that people can't handle freedom.'

'You're the notable exception. Do you know what you are? An authoritarian anarchist.'

I can't see. I must have put my glasses down somewhere. In a rising panic, I grope in the blur. Without my glasses I'm defenceless. I find them on the kitchen stove, an idiotic place to leave them, as stupid as on the chair. I sat on them, breaking one side, and the side is still held together with adhesive tape. With my glasses on I can see the dust, the fine grit that covers everything: the table, the stove, the unwashed dishes in the sink. And the place stinks. I wrinkle my nose. The toilet is blocked, I need a shower and dirty clothes have piled up in the laundry. They say your surroundings reflect your state of mind. I'm a mess. I must get myself out of this. I must fix the tank. The tin of sealer and a wooden dowel.

I whittle down the dowel and jam it into the hole, then seal it. A temporary job, but it will keep the water in until I get around to soldering the tank. I climb the ladder and unscrew the tank cover. The bottom is full of sludge, and on it floats one of Helga's ping-pong balls. She was always throwing her balls on the roof – 'Daddy, will you get my ball?' – I should boil my drinking water.

I rap the second tank. I haven't got a hose long enough to syphon the water from the one to the other. I'll wait until it cools down and use the bucket.

It is dark. I dread another night. And another day.

My back hurts, my arms are stiff. For hours I was a one-man bucket brigade, stooping, filling, lifting, balancing on the ladder, pouring water through the manhole; there is a foot of water in the large tank now. I've switched on the hot-water service and washed the dishes; I've flushed the toilet and soak in a tepid bath.

Cleaver didn't shoot at me.

The crickets are unusually loud tonight. Their concerted rattat-rattat drowns out the accursed jackpump in the valley.

I wish Cynthia was dead! For the first time, with a force that leaves me appalled and stunned, the wish for her death leaps into my mind. Cynthia's death will release me from my bondage, to her and to this godforsaken place. I will be free. I will win back Ingrid and my child!

Killing Cleaver I will enjoy: the look of surprise changing to terror on the meaty face, the thud of the bolt burying itself in his fat chest, his gasp of pain, the pain and the fear in his eyes dulling into the emptiness of death.

I will not enjoy killing Cynthia. I will kill her quickly, gently and with compassion. And afterwards I will arrange her broken little body in the peaceful posture of eternal sleep. And I will cry my eyes out in my loss and grief.

21

I DON'T think Cleaver has been back. At dawn, crossbow in hand, I searched for footprints on the hill, but the only marks in the dust by the barbed wire coils were those of my gumboots. He could lurk anywhere, of course, in the bush down by the road or across the valley and with his telescopic sight he could easily pick me off at a thousand metres. But no, he wouldn't kill me with a swift, deadly bullet out of the blue. He wants to prolong my terror, to see the fear in my eyes as I want to see the fear in his.

There's a letter from Vienna, from Resi. Since my father's death she has lived in the flat in the Eslarngasse alone, but she no longer plays the violin. Soon, she will move to a home for the aged. It will mean sharing a dormitory with fifteen other women. My father did not leave much: his viola, a stack of old theatre programmes, his gold signet ring with the green stone. She writes that she will welcome the company. Then the flat will have new tenants, another link with my past broken.

Frau Moser has died. It is with a pang of guilt and regret that I read of her death. I meant to write to her, or at least send a card, but I put it off too long.

She was my first love, a large woman with dimpled arms and a large laugh and rough hands that ruffled my hair. Frau Moser was everything my mother wasn't: earthy, physical, with a ripe sensuality that communicated itself to a boy of seven. She called me 'Bimpfi' after a character in a children's book and hugged me to her big breasts. I squirmed away and she laughed. She and Franzl, her husband, were the caretakers of our block of flats. She invited me in for glasses of Kracherl, a red raspberry drink that fizzed and spat. Franzl let me watch him build his model ships. He worked with infinite patience and attention to detail, bending over his tools at the kitchen table, carving, sandpapering, glueing, assembling hulls, spars, masts, rigging.

'Hey, Bimpfi, don't you go trampling all over my shiny floors.'

The bombs had begun to fall, but every day Frau Moser still polished the hall and the stairs and the brass buttons that summoned the lift. She had put down her mop and pail and sat on the steps. Her knees were parted wide and I stared up her skirt at her great dimpled thighs and a white strip of pants stretched over a softly rounded mound, disappearing into the crease between her buttocks. On her pants, below that mound, was a large, moist spot. My sexuality had not yet stirred, but I stared, fascinated, at that moist spot, at the contours so different from mine. She laughed and clapped her knees together. She reached out and tousled my hair.

For my mother, the human body did not exist between the neck and the knees. When she touched me it was always as if she was using her fingertips. She kissed me with her lips extended to keep as much distance as possible between us and warned me never to peep when she was in the bath or I would go blind. No wonder Frau Moser, who hugged me to her breasts and had a moist spot on her pants, excited and frightened me.

When I returned to Vienna, I rang Frau Moser's bell with a

beating heart. I had not forgotten the laugh and the ruffling hands and the raspberry sodas, nor the tingling sensuality. Now I was twenty-two.

Was this Frau Moser? She squinted up at me. Like everything here, she had shrunk, become smaller and older. 'It's me, Bimpfi,' I said uncertainly. Her blank stare turned to recognition. 'Bimpfi! Bimpfi!' She took my hand. 'I can't believe it. Come in. Come in!'

The flat had changed, become neglected. She moved a carton of empty bottles from a chair and cleared a space on the littered kitchen table. 'Your father said you were coming back, but I didn't recognise you. I still can't believe it. Will you have a glass of wine? Coffee?' Her joy was genuine, but she smelled of alcohol and her face was puffy. Her ripeness had turned to blowsiness. I asked for coffee. She put the kettle on and I accepted the greasy cup. I looked for Franzl.

'Franzl is back in hospital.' Her eyes dulled. 'It's his stomach again. Franzl has been ill for a long time. He's never been the same since the Russians took him away.'

She poured herself wine. 'He lost his job with the post office after the war because he was in the party. Franzl was never a Nazi, he didn't even know that he was in the party. A friend enrolled him in the party as a favour, without asking him, but after the war, the Russians came for him. I didn't hear from him for eight months, and he lost his job and his pension.'

I nodded. Could I believe that Franzl had never been a Nazi? Nazi Party memberships weren't given away. But he was harmless enough, quiet and kindly. He must have known of my mother's non-Aryan background; everyone here had known. He was just one of the thousands who had swum with the tide.

Her voice became bitter. 'The Russians brought a man called Schippral. Schippral went around with the Soviet commissars, pointing out Nazis. Franzl and I recognised him straight away. He was the same Schippral who went around with the SS pointing out Jews.'

I believed her about Schippral. The Schipprals were worse than the Franz Mosers.

'Schippral is still around, ' she said. 'He lives in the Juchgasse and works for the government. I bumped into him in the butcher's shop. He saw me and looked away. Schippral will get a pension.'

We talked a little longer, about other things, Australia. I finished the coffee and left heavy and sad. I went to London and my father wrote that Franzl had died of stomach cancer. I saw Frau Moser a few more times when I visited my father, but by then she was alcoholic, her eyes bloodshot, her face and figure bloated, her hair matted. She still cleaned the hall and the stairs and the lift, but the laughter was gone.

I carry Cleaver out to the car, first the newspaper-stuffed sack of a body, then the paperbag head. I prop him up behind the wheel, turn to the right, to the driver's-side door and adjust the head. I shut the door and open it, turn him a little more. I leave the door open.

I cock the crossbow, four bolts in the barrel. I have parked the car three feet from my garage. I position myself and run through the sequence: the sound of the approaching car; it stops at the gate, where the garage doors are now; the inside light goes on as he opens the car door; I step forward and make sure it is him; now, while he's turning in his seat to get out, at a disadvantage, clink! the bolt punches into his heart; three more bolts, clink! clink! clink!

Perfect. I pull out the bolts and run through the whole thing again. Now I'll have to practise at night.

I worry how I will kill Cynthia. With the crossbow? A bolt in the back of the neck at point-blank range? I'll never get away with it. But I must kill her if I am to be free.

I haven't worked on The Book for three days.

Mupp watches me. There is something in his round glass

eyes that I don't like. A tension has grown between us. In a moment he will speak again, let out one of his sarcastic remarks that I can do without. I pick him up, put him in the wardrobe and shut the door. I should have left him in his suitcase among the mothballs.

I listen to the sawing buzz of a blowfly, the recurring plunk as it hurls itself at the window pane. My arm hurts – blundering about without my glasses I banged into a door - and the bandage is crusted with dried blood. I should see a doctor, have a tetanus shot. I'll need a good right arm for what I have to do. Dr Hibberd in Mt Barker treated Ingrid and Helga, but I feel uncomfortable with him. He doesn't show it, but I know that he blames me for Ingrid's leaving – they all blame me for her leaving. I'll see a doctor in Adelaide. The casualty department at the Royal Adelaide is impersonal, anonymous.

I should write to Resi.

I should write to Resi, but I have nothing to say. No, what I do have to say she would never understand. Resi was kind to me when I returned to Vienna. She would be puzzled, disturbed, frightened, if she knew my mind. Resi would feel responsible for me, want to save me from myself. The thought of writing to her is too daunting – another of those empty letters that exclude everything: how are you, I'm fine, it must be winter in Vienna now, here it's hot . . . Our letters have become more and more infrequent. Resi is in her eighties. Soon, she too will be dead.

Since Ingrid left, I have cut myself off from everyone.

Insanity will be my defence. I shall evoke the bombs and the bullets, the little Jewish refugee with the pinched face under the large, flat cap. I shall play on their feelings of guilt about little Jewish boys with pinched faces under large, flat caps. I am, after all, the product of my genes - on the one hand, a decaying line of Austro-Hungarian aristocrats turned actors and musicians, on the other, centuries of inbreeding in the ghettos. There was my paternal grandfather, Zdenko, who could not accept the fall of the Habsburg monarchy. He booked the Royal Suite of Vienna's Imperial Hotel, locked the door, put on his blue uniform and sword, and after his pistol had misfired twice, opened the window and flung himself down to the pavement. And Uncle Oswald, my intended godfather, who was to have been given supervised leave from Steinhof for the christening, got away from his keepers the night before and leapt to his death. A quick replacement had to be found: Uncle Gottfried was chosen, a moody and solitary man, the author of obscure and highly academic tracts. He refused categorically to go into the shelter and was burned to death in his bed in the last raid on Vienna. And let us not forget Uncle Nathan, of the Jewish line, the brilliant bio-physicist who disappeared from his laboratory one day and was later found touring the nudist beaches of the world, writing and taking photographs for sunlovers' magazines.

The lechery of the Jew?

22

'I CRIED,' I tell Mupp.

I cried when I saw the boys in the park kill the mice. Not long afterwards, in the same park, I wrenched a toy petrol tanker away from another child who was playing with it in the sandbox. He looked at me in surprise. I carried the trophy back to my mother. 'Look what I found! I found it in the sand.' We went home, and I added the toy car to my collection. I was proud of myself. It was only later that I felt guilty.

'You were too young to know the difference between right and wrong.' For once, Mupp tries to console me. His spell in the wardrobe has made him contrite.

'But I did know the difference. I knew that what I was doing was wrong and cruel. I can still see the look in the boy's eyes, surprise, disbelief. And then his tears started to flow.'

'You've paid for it since.'

The Russian took my mouth organ. I was hiding in the hay. He ducked into the barn and saw me. Under his helmet, his face was broad and flat, his eyes glittering slits. His uniform was ragged and dirty, and he stank. He pointed his pistol at me and held out his free hand – he had watches strapped all up his forearm – he wanted my mouth organ. I gave it to him. He squatted in the hay beside me, playing my mouth organ with one hand and pointing his pistol with the other.

'See, you paid,' says Mupp.

'Did I? How does one small boy's loss and pain compensate for the loss and pain of the other?'

'You Germans started the war!' How often have I heard that argument used to justify the destruction of Vienna, Berlin, Frankfurt, Dusseldorf, Nuremberg, Dresden . . .

I started nothing! Hitler marched into Austria on my first birthday. I was two when the war broke out and six when the heavy raids on Vienna began. They were bombing *me*. I was below when the British and the Americans came in their Flying Fortresses in wave after wave, when they dropped their explosives to blow the roofs off the houses, and their incendiaries into the exposed timbers to create firestorms. Then they came back to machine-gun the fleeing people on the ground.

I was eight when the Russians shot at me. They wanted to kill the German in me, as the Nazis would have killed the Jew.

Rewind. Fast forward. Play. I run the video that is my life, backwards, forwards. I skip parts, stop here and there to freeze a frame.

I remember Gail, small, dark and cheeky, squatting on the roof of the playground shed, grinning, her legs wide apart, as I stood below. Her pants had worked themselves down and I could see right up into her; her pubic hair was just beginning to grow. I was desperately and tragically in love with her. When she missed school, my day was agony. I pictured her call for me as she lay in a fever, dying. Once I was bold enough to climb on her tram, to follow her home. She got off, turned a corner and disappeared before I could see the house. After that I haunted her neighbourhood, expecting to catch a glimpse of her through a hedge or a window, always afraid that her parents, or someone who knew me, would recognise me. When I heard that she had kissed Peter Cole, the golden-haired athlete, I writhed in jealousy for days.

Did it manifest itself even then, my need to love those who did not love me?

Ingrid loved me as I was. Perhaps that was why, in the end, I could not accept her love.

'Do you love me?' she pleaded. 'Please tell me that you love me.'

I remember the moment vividly: the blue tablecloth with its pattern of radishes, carrots, onions and tomatoes; her empty coffee cup; the full ashtray – she smoked far too much – the anxiety in her eyes, crying out for reassurance. I should have taken her in my arms and held her close, I should have said, 'I love you.' I wanted to, but I could not.

Later, I accepted Cynthia's protestations of love. Did I know, deep down, that she did not really love me, that to her it was all a game? I noticed her touch of cruelty: in the way she treated others and spoke about them; her indifference to her dog; her capriciousness and unreliability.

Ingrid's tablecloth is still on the table, but the waxed surface is worn, the pattern has faded. Above the chair where she sat, the ceiling is stained brown from her smoking.

115

The video. Stop. Rewind. Fast forward. Play.

Swastika flags are flying in Vienna on this a cold, bright winter morning. My mittened hand is in my father's. We are walking and the flags are bright red, white and black. A military band is playing. The winter sun glints on the brass. I am fascinated by the trombone players, swallowing the tubes, and by the big bass drum: boom! boom!

At the sideshows in the Prater, boys pitch leather balls at the hats of papier-mache heads. 'Knock his block off!' they yell.

I am with my mother in a crowded shop, and I point at the bust of Hitler on a shelf above the counter. 'Knock his block off!' I am too young to understand her terror.

But her fear transmitted itself to me, subtly infiltrating me day after day. A tension, a vague foreboding, gripped me even before the bombs began to fall. A terror that has never left me shaped and became part of me. It ebbs and flows, sometimes simmering away deep in my gut and then rising to choke me. I have found temporary refuge from it with a woman, between her thighs.

And I have sought to master the terror by becoming one with its creator. In megalomanic euphoria, I would see myself, one hand at the buckle of my belt, the other raised in salute, striding to the rostrum below the banners and the eagles to announce my mission to a trembling world, my ears filled not with my voice and my words, but with the rough, guttural cadences of Adolf Hitler, and then with the thunderous ovation of the mesmerised crowd.

Before us lies Germany, in us marches Germany, behind us comes Germany!

Sieg Heil! Sieg Heil! Sieg Heil . . .

'Hitler is Germany,' shouts Hess, 'and Germany is Hitler.'

Hitler is in me. And I am in Hitler. He is my Jesus, as Christ is to the Christians.

I see the pale mountains of corpses at Auschwitz. But I suppose the churches burned thousands in Jesus Christ's name, in the name of love.

I should have thought of it before: I must get some ammonium nitrate fertiliser. Mix a capful of diesel oil into a bucketful of the fertiliser and you have an explosive that will blow tree stumps out of the ground. I will lay a minefield around the house so that if Cleaver returns, the ground under him will erupt in dirt and fire.

But to set the stuff off, you need a detonator, a primer, gelignite and a fuse. You can't buy them over the counter; questions are asked and records kept. Perhaps I can steal them from a quarry or from a highways department or railways store. A length of iron pipe filled with black powder and plugged at both ends may do the job. So will a high-velocity rifle bullet, fired from six inches of steel tubing of the right diameter, using a simple trigger set off by a tripwire.

On scraps of paper, I scribble diagrams. A two-inch nail compressed against a coil spring will make an effective striker, fixed by a pin attached to the wire.

Euphoric now, I reach for more paper. My sketches cover the table. I feel better. I am on top of things. I am in control of my life.

Since 5.45 this morning, we have been shooting back, and from now on, we will retaliate, bomb for bomb . . .

Sieg Heil! Sieg Heil . . .

I sat in the press gallery, my pad on my knees, and studied the faces of the ten shabby men in the dock. Otto Kaiser: life imprisonment. Friedrich Mayerhof: twenty years. Karl Kunne: fifteen years. Hans Drescher: ten years. Eberhard Sturm: ten years . . . Only the twitch of a jaw muscle or an eyelid betrayed their emotions. What was it like to live with their consciences and their memories? A few years later, all would be free again. Their victims stayed dead.

'Bomber' Harris, whose planes rained death from the skies to tear limb from limb or burn alive 600,000 civilian men, women and children in Vienna, Berlin, Hamburg, Frankfurt, Dusseldorf, Nuremberg, Dresden, was elevated to the peerage.

MARS IN SCORPIO

Kaiser and Harris. You could say that each acted from the best of motives. The one would have murdered me to purify the race, the other tried his best to kill me to save me from Kaiser.

Larry and the charge attendant were free of all ideology. Their only cause was the innocent pursuit of fun.

'You're a dirty bastard, aren't you, Westie?'

'OWOOOH!'

When sentence was pronounced in that courtroom in Cologne on the ten shabby men, I thought of Larry and the charge attendant.

And I saw myself kicking Weston in the shins. The charge attendant and Larry and I should have stood in the dock with Sturm and Drescher and Kunne and Mayerhof and Kaiser...

The charge attendant had a way of making Roy Driver mad. Driver hated the sight of him, when he saw him he spat out 'bastard' under his breath.

The charge attendant kept a straight face and murmured 'bastard' back at him from the corner of his mouth. Driver expanded it to, 'Ahrr, you bastard, you cunt, bastard yourself.' The charge attendant continued to look innocently ahead and, without moving his lips, repeated, 'Ahrr, bastard, cunt, bastard yourself.' In less than a minute, he got Driver so worked up that Driver leapt up and down like a jumping dervish, yelling and cursing at the top of his lungs.

'You never worked in your lives, you bastards! Making your livings sticking needles into a man! Let me tell you, I know what work is, you cunts! I fought in two world wars. I killed men, you bastards, I killed better men than you...'

The charge attendant and Larry had a shaving race. At stake was a crate of beer. The bet was who could shave more patients in five minutes. The word had spread, and all the attendants who

118

could get away came to watch. Big Hanson from the Imbecile Ward agreed to referee. The charge attendant won the toss for the first pick. He chose Jonesy for his nicely rounded cheeks. Larry picked McNaughton. They waited, razors poised, as Hanson counted down the seconds, 'Ten, nine, eight, seven, six...' Jonesy blinked nervously, aware that something wasn't quite as it should be. At 'zero!' they swooped. The charge attendant used long and rapid strokes, down, up and down the left cheek, from left to right under the nose, right cheek, chin, throat, towel over the face and a hoist and a shove, to send Jonesy, spluttering but unmarked, on his way. Larry finished a split second later to accompanying cheers.

Larry grabbed Babinski, and the charge attendant shaved Ford, and they remained neck and neck. Scraping away furiously, Larry finished the next one ahead, but then he made a mistake and got hold of Driver who protested, 'You bastards aren't going to fuck around with me' and knocked over shaving mug and chair. Encouraged by an enthusiastic audience, Larry tried to fight Driver down. Driver ripped open Larry's shirt. They spun into the charge attendant, who cut a piece out of Weston's chin. Weston went, 'WOOOHOO!'

All out to regain his lead, Larry laid open Kowalski's lip. Blood and lather ran into Kowalski's collar.

'What's all this?' The senior attendant had arrived unannounced.

'Driver went off his nut,' the charge attendant said.

23

M Y NEED for a woman is reawakened; sex, and the urge to kill. I have fantasies of Cynthia on the white shagpile rug, voracious in orgasm, her teeth bared, but the meaty face of the hated Cleaver intervenes and I beat his head to a bloody pulp on the floor. From sex back to violence.

There are two letters left unanswered: one from Phyllis, the widow with the two teenage sons, the other from Carol, the full-time student with three growing daughters. Why start a family when you can acquire one ready-made? Carol is a big blonde, with big breasts, big dimpled arms and big dimpled thighs, like Frau Moser. The three daughters, well-developed for their age, are precocious, images of their mother. All four of them, sex-crazed, are waiting to tear off my pants for an orgy of intertwined bodies, sweat, saliva, vaginal juices, my spurting semen . . . I pick up the phone. I am naked but for the bandage on my arm and I have an erection.

Nobody answers.

Fuck!

Phyllis has two teenage sons. No thought of an orgy with them – I'm not that way. I try to see myself kicking a football around the backyard but don't quite succeed. Perhaps they'll leave home, get the dole. Anyway, I don't want to marry the woman. I need sex.

I lift the phone again. Phyllis's number.

'He-ll-o-o?'

Her voice charged with female sexuality excites me. My erection quivers.

'I'm the author. I advertised. I received your letter.'

A pause. 'How nice of you to call.'

She's still interested! 'It's hard to talk on the phone. I thought, perhaps, we could meet over coffee...'

'Why not?'

'What about the Cafe Boulevard? Can you come to the city?'

'Why don't you come here?'

An invitation to her home! I try not to sound too eager! Yes, I would like to come. When?

'Why not this afternoon. Around four?'

Her address is in Kensington Gardens, one of the better suburbs. Something occurs to me. 'Your boys. Would they mind?'

She laughs, a low laugh vibrating with the same sexuality. 'Don't worry about them. I don't let the boys interfere with my life. Anyway, Justin is away at camp.'

It is after two. I will have to hurry. A clean shirt, clean shorts. I have no clean shorts. The electric razor won't work again. I bang it against the wall. Where is the deodorant? My erection is a nuisance. Not now, boy, down! down!

The house is pretentious, one of those solid, double-fronted houses built in the thirties, with birdbath and goldfish pond and sprinklers sweeping the rolling lawn. The door chimes tinkle the opening bars of *Waltzing Matilda*. Phyllis is tiny, the top of her carefully ringleted and red-tinted head no higher than my second shirt button. Two berry eyes peer up at me from a crinkled face. Her lipstick is too crimson and there is a smear of it on her front teeth. She leads me along the hall, past a tall vase on a marble-topped table, over oriental rugs scattered on the brightly polished floor. I sit on the chintz-covered sofa in the eggshell-blue lounge room. Cool air whispers from the ceiling. I am uncomfortably aware of the wet patches below the armpits of my shirt, the limpness of my shorts, the tired bandage on my arm. Over the mantel hangs a large, framed photograph of a broad-shouldered man in a dark business suit. He has a high forehead, close-set blue eyes and a long chin.

'Tea? Coffee? Campari with Coke?' I ask for Campari and she leaves me with the photograph. We regard each other uneasily, the photograph and I. She returns with tall frosted glasses on a silver tray, which she places on the glass coffee table at my knees. She is wearing loose pants of maroon towelling and a short-sleeved, pink cotton top. She is built like a child, thin arms, slightly freckled, no hips, no arse. She clambers on the sofa beside me.

'Tell me about yourself.' Her leg touches mine, her upturned face is very close. My glance is drawn back to the picture. 'My husband, an accountant,' she explains. 'Sinclair was killed in a plane crash sixteen years ago. We were married for less than two years.''

I murmur something that I hope is appropriate. What do you say to someone whose husband was killed in a plane crash, even if it was sixteen years ago? Sinclair's close-set blue gaze unsettles me, as do the eggshell-blue walls, the closeness of her face, her crimson lips, the lipstick smear on her front teeth.

'I never married again. Oh, I've had relationships, but it's so difficult to find the right person. Still, one needs the opposite sex, don't you think?'

The door flies open and in bursts a muscular youth with an earring and a wet towel round his waist. 'Sorry, mum.' He disappears again, but not before he gives me a disapproving look with his close-set blue eyes. 'Don't drip on the floors,' she calls. A moment later, the beat of drums throbs through the house.

'Warren plays in a band,' she says indulgently. 'He's seventeen and very like his father.'

I sip my Campari. She sees my bandage. 'What have you done to your arm?'

'It's only a cut.'

'Let me look at that for you. I was a nurse, you know. Come to the bathroom.'

The bathroom is all mirrors. Warren has left puddles on the tiles. She sighs. She unwinds the gauze. The last bit sticks to the hairs on my arm. She tugs it off and I wince. 'That's healing nicely. You won't need this anymore.' She drops the soiled bandage into the bin. 'It should have air.'

I'm disappointed. No martyrdom for me. I'm not going to die of blood poisoning or lose my arm.

'I'll show you the rest of the house.' I find myself in a white bedroom dominated by a huge brass four-poster heaped with ruffled cushions. Suddenly, she is pressing against me, her arms around my neck, pulling me down, the crimson mouth seeking mine. Her breath tastes bitter. My hands are at her waist, peeling down her pants. Over her shoulder, I see the photo on the bedside table: Sinclair again, with the close-set blue stare. She slips off her top and her bra, her small breasts and her belly are loose. I step out of my shorts and kick off my shoes. Then she is under me on the bed, but I see only the late Sinclair's eyes and hear the throb, throb of Warren's drums. I've lost my erection. I try and try, but I can't get it in. She grabs me and pumps and squeezes with rising anger and frustration, but it doesn't help.

We dress in silence. She looks at her watch. 'I'm expecting guests for dinner.' She wants me to go, and I want to leave. She escorts me to the door. Goodbye, Phyllis. I walk out of the house without a backward glance.

The buzz of the blowfly, the plunk, plunk, as it hurls itself against the pane haunts me. I am trapped, like that blowfly. I want to ram my head into the walls until I shatter the fibro-cement sheets and mash my brains.

Red rising fury grips me. Sex was offered to me on a platter, but I couldn't perform. I curse myself. I curse Cynthia. I curse Cleaver.

The bastard! I know tonight he'll be there, I know it. The moment of our fatal rendezvous has come. The pistol is loaded, powder in the pan and the flint clamped tight. I flex the crossbow. The four bolts are in place.

I wait in the shadows in Launder Avenue, the bow in my hand, the pistol heavy in my belt. It is getting dark. I hear the sound of a motor. A car. Cleaver's? Dazzling headlights approach. Resolve. *Die Fahne Hoch . . .!* The car pulls up, and the driver's door opens. I step forward. It is Cleaver, I meant to get him in his seat. He faces me out of the car. I level the bow and squeeze off a bolt. He has me by the wrists, and we struggle for the bow, but he is stronger than me. I knee him in the groin and he drops. I can't recock the bow. I draw the pistol. He snatches the muzzle. I wrench it away and smash it in his face. The force jars my arm. I thumb back the cock and jerk the trigger. A long flash of red flame. The ball grazes his jaw. He is on all fours in the beam of the headlights, his jaw hanging loose. He grabs my legs, and I reverse the gun and drive it into the back of his head. His arms lock. I try to kick him away, club him again and again. Bone crunches, and he gurgles. Blood, hot and wet, covers my glasses. I strike blindly. He goes limp. I hear voices, I turn and run, pulling off my glasses as I go. I've lost the bow. I reach the car and fling my glasses and the pistol inside. The starter grinds, the engine kicks, and I take off, tyres screaming.

Now for Cynthia! The road is a blur. I stop, my glasses! I wipe the blood off them and put them on. I'm soaked in blood. I thrash through the gears. Right at Fullarton Road, right into Wattle Street, left, then right again. I screech into her driveway. One car in the carport, the Lamborghini. I hammer on the front door. Damn it, I know she's there. Open up! I pound on the door with the pistol butt. I'll crash my way in. The door opens. Cynthia stands there, like a ghost, eyes glassy and unfocused, she's spaced out, on Valium, Serepax, Mogadon or God knows what. I push past her and walk, shoes bloodied, on to the white shagpile.

'I've killed the bastard!'

She looks at me blankly.

'I've killed him! Cleaver!' I shake her like a rag doll, my hands leave red prints on her white gown. Damn, damn, I want her to understand, but it's no good, nothing registers. I've come to kill her, but I want her to know first what I've done. I want her to know that Cleaver is dead and why she has to die too. It's all gone wrong. The crossbow's lost, and there's no time to reload the pistol. I'll batter her to death with the empty gun, one well-placed blow with the brass-bound butt, sticky with Cleaver's blood. But I can't do it, I just know I can't do it. She's tottered to the couch and sits there, face vacant, hands loose in her lap. I go into the kitchen and find a carving knife, long and sharp, I approach her from behind. I kiss the nape of her neck. 'I've always loved you,' I whisper. Then I draw the blade across her throat.

I place my hands around her neck, thumbs and index fingers on the carotids and jugulars, and squeeze.

I grasp a handful of hair, the silken, blue-black hair, and jerk her head back until her spine snaps.

I dissolve all the pills in her medicine cabinet and force her to drink, then hold her hand as she drifts away.

Jack stands in the door. I freeze, the knife at Cynthia's throat. He raises his pistol, aims and shoots.

24

'THAT WOULD be too easy,' gibes Mupp. 'For Jack to kill you. Do you really think life's solutions are as simple as that?' He is back in the wardrobe, but I can still hear his voice.

I press my hands to my ears, but his laughter reverberates in the echo chamber of my skull.

'I hate you,' I sob.

'That's because you only love those who would destroy you.'

He is right. I loved Cynthia, who ate like woodworm into the fibres of my soul; I love Hitler, who would have gassed me; and Ingrid I did not love enough, because she loved me selflessly, was constant and faithful, because she wanted the best for me.

To Cynthia I was never more than a diversion, a pawn to be manipulated, played off against Jack and Cleaver; my attentions flattered her. I gratified her, fool that I was, and allowed her to act out her fantasies of power. My love for Hitler has been a dark one, uneasy and Orwellian, the pale mountains of corpses in the death camps always in the background. In London, members of the British Nazi Party were selling their literature in the street. I bought and read their newspaper and pamphlets. I despised them. They loved Hitler because of the gas chambers. It is my curse to love him despite them.

Hitler, born on the cusp of Aries and Taurus, his Sun conjunct my Venus. Is that the reason for the dark bond?

To love Hitler is to loathe that part of me he would never accept. Only when I have exterminated the Jew in me will Hitler return my love.

'You cannot exterminate the Jew in you without exterminating yourself,' says Mupp, always the voice of reason. 'Anyway, you don't really believe all that Nazi racist rubbish. There is no such thing as "the Jew in you". You might as well believe in the doctrine of original sin.'

'Speaking rationally, you're quite right.'

'You always said that no idea, ideology or belief is worth burning anyone at the stake for, that man is an animal, a mammal, an ape, that he should accept his apehood and forget his superstitions and delusions of grandeur, that the only good in him is the simple good of his apehood, the need to give and to receive warmth, to nurture . . .'

'Yes, I said that.'

'Then why not live accordingly?'

'Because I have been bent, twisted, perverted,' I scream. 'I have been alienated from myself. I know the schizophrenia of the indoctrinated, the mind at war with itself, reason pitted against conditioning.'

'You are like all the rest of you,' Mupp says sadly. 'That's why you will all blow yourselves up.'

We will all blow ourselves up, or choke in the filth of our civilisation. 'Daddy, I know I won't live to be an adult,' said Helga. Most of her schoolmates believed that they wouldn't live to be adults. Helga is growing up in the midst of plenty: she has a ghetto-blaster as big as a house, her own colour TV, and when she is hungry, there is food in the fridge. The planes overhead carry passengers, not bombs; the houses have roofs and windows; the Gestapo does not knock at dawn to take her mother away.

Does it matter if I never recreate my book? Who will be there to read it? I planted a tree and it was consumed by fire. The result of every act of creation is doomed to destruction. Monuments crumble, books turn to dust, beauty withers and dies. I have written a book, planted a tree and fathered a child, and nothing will remain of all three. But if I destroy the Mona Lisa – or murder a man – my act will stand for ever.

A cockroach sits by the skirting board, flat, shiny, motionless, waiting. Does it sense, somewhere in its minuscule brain, that its day is coming? Unchanged by time since the dawn of life, it will survive radiation, nuclear winter, the greenhouse effect and acid rain. The extinction of the dinosaurs made way for the mammals, the ascent of man. Our extinction will make way for the insects. The age of the cockroach will begin.

I raise my foot to stamp it into the floorboards, then change my mind. Perhaps it is already sitting in judgement on me.

The four horsemen of the Apocalypse are coming. I can hear the distant thunder of the hooves. And the jackpump.

One letter is left. Carol, who has three daughters and large, dimpled arms, big breasts and dimpled thighs – Frau Moser – Carol will save me.

The line is out of order.

I try again.

I ring Telecom.

'The number has been disconnected.'

Another thread of hope severed. Anyway, Carol was probably not like Frau Moser at all. Most likely, she was small and thin and brittle, like Phyllis with the ringleted and too-red tinted hair.

I try Cynthia whose slender throat I cut, whose fragile neck I snapped, whom I poisoned with the contents of her medicine cabinet.

No answer.

The rest home. Mrs Beazley. 'May I speak to the Reverend Cleaver?' Cleaver, whom I battered to a bloody pulp, has not returned.

A blank sheet sits in the dusty typewriter.

Panic grips me.

The horsemen come nearer.

I will kill the Jew in me. I will complete Hitler's work, and then, at last, Hitler will return my love. And then I will no longer need Cynthia, nor Ingrid. Only the Jew in me stands between me and his love.

Winston Smith loved Big Brother. Did Big Brother love Winston Smith?

The Jew in me, my incubus, the nasty little Kike who will not go away, lives between my fourth and fifth ribs, and sometimes comes out to jeer at me. I recognise him at once. I have read my Diebow and Hans F. K. Guenther: the Jewish nose, 'a long, thin convex type of nose with a marked or barely perceptible hump on the bridge', which is not Israelite but Armenoid, the result of the bastardisation of the Israelites with Hittites and other brachycephalic peoples who penetrated

Palestine from the Anatolian plateau; the flat feet; the legs short in relation to the spine; the negroid lips expressing the lustful sensuality of the Jew, and within him, vampire-like, the Jewish racial soul, waiting to feast on the jugular of the Aryan race.

I will smite him as I smote Israel Fish.

In Hamburg, on the waterfront, The Captain presides over his labyrinth of sixteen junk-filled rooms. You descend half a dozen steps and skirt a basket of dried boxfish to squeeze inside. A crude but effective hand-lettered sign warns shoplifters of The Captain's vengeance; a crude sketch of The Captain, bald and with a ferocious black beard, lends weight to the warning. Behind the counter, even more impressive, is The Captain himself, the domed and shiny pate, black eyes under bushy brows, and a matted beard that reaches halfway down his barrel chest.

He nods to me. I have bought things from him before – netsukes and a Melanesian devil's mask and a skull carved from bone – and sometimes we have talked. The Captain trades in everything seamen bring him: carved ivory, coins, barbed spears, boomerangs, African fetishes, Balinese masks, Javanese shadow puppets, joss sticks, brass Buddhas, saris and sarongs, stuffed baby crocodiles, old ships' lanterns and fishing nets, dried and shrivelled objects that smell of the sea. From one room to another my progress is interrupted by cases of seashells and mouldering books. The mounted head of a tiger shark, mouth full of triangular teeth, grins at me from close quarters. I encounter an iron maiden, not for sale, once a theatre prop, convincingly sculpted from styrofoam. One room is filled with military memorabilia, German steel helmets, an SS officer's tunic on a stand, dusty boxes of badges, insignia, ribbons and medals. I find a curiously shaped piece of cloth about the size of my palm and smooth it out, a six-pointed star. Once yellow, it is dirty and faded. The embroidered letters, still legible, say *Jude*, Jew.

I stare at the relic, shudder. The star in my hand, I retrace my steps to the front of the shop. The Captain is trying to interest a potential buyer in an Arab dagger, the curved blade glinting wickedly in the dim light. I stand and wait. The Captain wraps the dagger, the cash register chimes, the customer departs with his purchase. I put the star on the counter. The Captain looks at it with a frown.

'I don't know how that got in there.' He picks it up with two pointed fingers, reluctant to touch it, and is about to drop it into a drawer.

I stop him. 'I'll buy it. How much?'

The Captain holds it out between his stubby fingers. 'Take it.'

I put it in the pocket of my overcoat. I turn to leave and glance over my shoulder. The Captain seems glad to see me go.

Outside, in the Bernhard-Nocht-Strasse, the girls stand in the doorways of the crumbling tenements. I nod to a stringy blonde, and follow her into her room. She stuffs the thirty marks into her handbag without even going through the routine of haggling. She hoists her skirt, steps out of her pants, two pairs to keep her warm, and lies on the rumpled bed. I am glad that she does not talk. I purge myself, we dress and go downstairs together without exchanging another word, and she resumes her cold vigil in the doorway.

I take the steps down the embankment and stand by the black water of the Elbe. A ship slides past, heading out to sea, black bulk, a row of lit portholes, an ocean-going freighter. A foghorn sounds mournfully and I hear music coming from a tavern on the Fischmarkt. I head for the U-Bahn Landungsbrucken.

It is after midnight when I return to my apartment. I slump in a chair and remove my shoes, take the star from the pocket of my overcoat and look at it with a mixture of revulsion and fascination. Something makes me step to the mirror and hold it to my breast. Jew. A chill finger touches my spine.

In the kitchen, over the sink, I strike a match and touch it to one of the points. The material burns badly, it smokes and the match goes out. I light another: more black smoke, the smell of burning cloth. The match scorches my thumb and I drop it into the sink. Singed, the star looks more obscene than before. My flesh crawls. I light one of the gas rings. Now it is alight. The word *Jude* pales and disappears, ash and glowing threads drift away. I have to blow out the flames before they reach my fingers, but one point remains. I go to the bathroom and drop it in the lavatory, but I have to flush twice before it washes down the drain. I hold my hand under the tap, to soothe the burn, washing away the star.

'You should kill the Hitler in yourself,' says Mupp, 'not the Jew.'

25

HOW CAN I kill the Hitler in myself, or the Jew? Especially now that the Jews have taken on all the characteristics of Hitler. Ariel Sharon let the Lebanese Christians slaughter Palestinian women and children in the refugee camps: the Butcher of Beirut. And Sharon is still around.

It is said that Himmler's number two man, the feared Reinhard Heydrich, tall, blond, athletic, musical prodigy and expert swordsman, creator of the SS security apparatus and co-architect of the final solution, was part-Jewish. Himmler, of course, knew of Heydrich's Jewish blood, and it gave him a hold over him. When Heydrich was assassinated, Himmler had a death mask made of him and hung it in his office. 'Heydrich suffered intensely,' said Himmler. 'I often talked to him and tried to help him. In spite of my own convictions I tried to make him believe that it was possible to overcome partly Jewish blood thanks to the superiority of the German strain. At the time he seemed grateful for my help, and relieved, but never for long.'

A joke circulated about Heydrich's self-loathing: One night, Heydrich came home drunk and saw himself in the mirror. He drew his pistol and emptied the magazine into the mirror, shouting, 'Got you at last, you swine!'

I have a picture of Heydrich from a newspaper, which I look at: he has a long head and face, jutting ears, close-set reptilian eyes, a long nose, a sensual but cruel mouth, and a face that radiates a cold intelligence and ruthless ambition. A Jewish face? Heydrich wanted to exterminate the Jew in himself, but instead he exterminated the Jews.

I am guilty.

I herded the victims into the gas chambers. I tossed in tins of Zyklon B and listened to the screams and the choking.

I drove the Palestinians from their lands. I unleashed the murderers on the refugee camps.

By virtue of my species I am guilty of every crime committed by man since Cain slew Abel. I am guilty of the extermination of other life forms. I am guilty of the pollution of the skies and of the waters. I am guilty of turning the continents into deserts.

I am guilty of the coming holocaust.

I am guilty, and I am trapped. I cannot atone for my guilt. I continue to pollute and to exterminate.

I am doomed.

The horsemen of the Apocalypse are coming.

We did not create the world, said Hitler, we must deal with it as it is.

I did not create the world. Why do I feel guilty?

We do not idealise people, said Goebbels, all men are not equal, some are good and some are worthless.

I did not create mankind. Then why do I feel guilty?

I want to be free, free of guilt. Free of Hitler and of the Jew. Free of Cynthia and of Cleaver. I want to break their power over me that only I have granted them. Sanity and survival demand it. But the passions that burn in my gut defy all reason.

A blowfly buzzes around the room and lands on the blind, fat, black and hairy.

Am I good or worthless?

Goebbels said:

'The Jews are people too – as if we ever said otherwise. The same is true of murderers, child molesters, thieves and pimps. There is a difference between people and people, just as there is a difference between animals and animals. We know good and bad people, as we know good and bad animals. The fact that the Jew still lives among us does not mean that he belongs to us, just as the flea does not become a domestic animal because we find it in the house.'

'You don't really believe that you're a flea?' Mupp says.

'I don't know what I believe.'

'You know that Hitler isn't God.'

'They took Hitler away from me. What would a Christian say if they took away his Christ? If he was told, Christ is a war criminal? In Australia, the parents of a school friend took me to church. Over the altar hung a big picture of Jesus, one of those effeminate Jesuses in a long purple robe. I wanted to tear down that Jesus. I wanted to put Hitler in his place. Why should they have their Jesus when I wasn't allowed to have my Hitler?'

'Their Jesus had nothing to do with the real Jesus, just as your Hitler has nothing to do with the real Hitler. Remember that newsreel of Hitler at the Olympic Games? A little man with a crooked mouth under the Chaplin moustache, jumping up and down on his seat and kneading his knee. You always hated that newsreel, didn't you? Because that jumping Hitler kneading his knee threatened your image of Hitler, the God.'

I say nothing.

'You can forgive Hitler the gas chambers in which you might have been gassed, but you can't forgive him for jumping up and down on his seat and kneading his knee.'

Gods can kill, but they don't knead their knees. I try not to think of Hitler kneading his knee. I still need Hitler.

The blowfly preens itself on the blind. Outside, in the valley, the jackpump clunks and shrieks. I hate the jackpump more than I hate the nuclear arsenal that is waiting to blow up the world.

I detest Cleaver more than I detest the generals in the Kremlin and the Pentagon.

I fear the past more than I fear the future.

I aim the flyspray at the blowfly, which sits on the blind and preens itself, unaware. I give it a puff. It hums to the ceiling, then spirals to the floor. It spins around and around on the carpet, its wings still humming. The spinning stops, its wings are still.

For the fly, the past and the future have become irrelevant.

In the bedroom stands the piano, the old upright *Bucher* with the delicately turned columns. It has a dark sound, and some of the keys are sticking. I bought it at an auction because it is a beautiful thing and then was told that it is worthless because it has no iron frame. The lid is covered with the red, gritty dust; I have not opened it for a year. Now I sit at the keyboard and hammer out the Horst Wessel Song in ever new variations. I bawl the words, the sweat pours down my face.

And when the Jewish blood runs from the knife . . .

I have shouted myself hoarse. I slam the lid. The instrument reverberates like a choir in hell.

I must write to Resi. I haven't seen her for fifteen years. Now she is in her eighties. I remember her as small, dark, sturdy, always cheerful. We walked in the Vienna Woods, stumping along under the enormous rucksack that she insisted on carrying, holding enough provisions for a regiment: bread, cheese, sausage, thermos flask, glass jars full of her home-made potato salad, mugs and plates, warm pullovers, my father's spare hiking boots. We always ate at an inn, my father never needed his spare boots and Resi cheerfully carried the whole load home again.

Resi still has my father's heavy gold signet ring with the family coat of arms engraved in the green stone. I want to wear it, but she ignores all the references to the ring in my letters. Surely she hasn't sold it or lost it? Once she goes into the nursing home, I'll never see the ring again because, when she dies, the nurses or the cleaners will take it.

I have nothing that belonged to my father. When I was young, I only saw him seldom, although because he was an entertainer he was not called up until the end of the war. He was of a male generation that simply did not know what to do with small children. The few times he took me anywhere stand out in my memory: the afternoon in the Military Museum, an outing to the Wurstelprater, Vienna's fun fair, where we rode on the ghost train. I will never forget that ride: the car jerking forwards on its rail to bang through the swinging doors, the skeletons, devils and witches leaping at us out of the dark. When I returned to Vienna, we went to the Wurstelprater and rode all the ghost trains. The old Wurstelprater had been destroyed in the last days of the war and the original ghost train was gone. Half a dozen new ones replaced it, each grander than the last, but those who remember say that the Wurstelprater has never been the same.

Was it because I had so little of my father that I turned to Hitler? My only other male model was my Jewish stepfather, who made me stand at attention while he reached out and smashed me in the face.

My father is dead, my stepfather, the terror of my teens, is a senile travesty of himself. He shuffles about in a soiled dressing gown and pyjamas, almost totally deaf, incontinent,

135

mumbling to himself between asthmatic wheezes. My mother and he have detested each other for forty years. Old age has dampened their continual warfare: he poisoned her favourite trees and put the sprinkler across the path when she was due back from a neighbour's. She turned the cold water on full when he was under the shower.

'I have truly hated only two people,' my mother said. 'One was Hitler, and the other is your stepfather.' My mother has become brittle and bitter, her dreams, too, have been shattered, and now her time is running out. She knows that she will never reach the Promised Land.

'One way traffic' was one of my stepfather's favourite phrases. He meant that he gave generously because I ate his food and lived in his house, and I gave nothing in return. The Saturday afternoons spent pulling couch grass from his lawn did not count. My brother and I pulled couch grass from the lawn together, and, despite the seven years between us, were very close. My stepfather insisted on taking us to the synagogue, and I watched the alien ritual, the bearded figures in their long, black caftans swaying and chanting. It was the Jews at Hofgastein all over again, and I felt violated and threatened. I refused to go again.

From remnants of cloth I sewed the great swastika flag which I defiantly hung on the wall over the head of my bed.

Swastika flags, black, white and red,
Waving and calling: Be true unto death!

My stepfather saw the flag and ripped it to pieces. I never did comprehend how much cause he had to hate that symbol. Later I discovered that the old man was not all bad; he was not one of the educated, cultured Jews who might have influenced me quite differently. He could not overcome his background in a poverty-stricken village in Slovakia.

My brother and I have lost contact – he has become an entrepreneur and goes his own way – and I seldom see my mother. I have become a recluse in this empty house in the sun-scorched hills, alone with the clunk-shriek of the pump and my obsession with the past. And with Cynthia and Cleaver.

Before me on the kitchen table, deadly, lie the crossbow and the pistol.

26

'ARE YOU SURE you can kill?' asks Mupp. 'Are you sure you can do it? Are you sure you are up to the bloody work of it? It takes stomach to kill. Do you have the stomach for it?'

I try to ignore the voice from the wardrobe.

'It takes stomach,' echoes Cleaver. 'Stomach, stomach, stomach . . .'

'Remember the cat,' persists Mupp, 'the bloodied cat, writhing on the road? You hit it with the brick again and again . . .'

'The policeman finally killed the cat,' taunts Cleaver. 'You couldn't do it.'

'They poisoned Rasputin,' says Mupp. 'They shot him. And he still lived; they threw him in the river.'

'It's not easy to kill,' jeers Cleaver. 'You have to have stomach, stomach.'

'I almost killed Fish! I hit him and hit him and hit him while the blood poured from his head!'

'But cold, premeditated murder? Could you really kill Cynthia?' Cleaver is mocking me. 'You say you love her.'

'There is nothing I can do to Cynthia that she has not already done to me.'

Cynthia liked to twist the knife.

I was upset. 'Where were you last night? You said you'd be home. I phoned. I tried to reach you all evening.'

'Oh, I had dinner with Christian.' She looked for my reaction. It came, a tightening of my jaw. One–nil to her. Her dark eyes were big, innocent, shining.

I said nothing.

'He really is the most awful bore.' Her fingers played with my shirt buttons. She nestled against me like a kitten. Now that she had planted the knife, right where it hurt me most, she put Cleaver down. 'I don't know why I bother with him. I suppose it is because the poor man is so pathetic.' But the knife was in, a sharp pain just below my sternum. And then the twist. I should have been prepared for the twist from previous occasions. But she always caught me off guard.

'Christian really did annoy me. Because he said something very insulting about you. I really shouldn't tell you this.' Her eyes were on me again, dark and expectant.

I gritted my teeth and remained silent.

'He said you remind him of *The Great Dictator*.'

'*The Great Dictator*?' I bit, in spite of myself.

'Yes, Charlie Chaplin playing Hitler.'

Two–nil. Even if he did say it, there was no need to tell me. Another look from the dark eyes. Had she gone too far? She withdrew the knife, soothed the wound with her protestations of love. We went to bed. I discharged what remained of my anger into her.

What remained of my anger? No, with each episode, more and more anger built up inside me, a sickness like a cancer.

'We've booked a beach house at Port Broughton and now Jack has to fly to Hong Kong. Would you like to come? We'll be all alone there. Just you and me.'

I didn't hear from her for a week. She had gone to Port Broughton with Cleaver.

I turned all my hatred against the Reverend Cleaver, the adulterous Man of God, the mealy-mouthed hypocrite, Rasputin. But it is Cynthia I should have hated.

But I need Cynthia as I need Hitler.

'You never touch me any more,' Ingrid said.

It was true. I hadn't touched her since the fire. It was the breaking point. The first fire, that is. The second sealed our fate: the end of our marriage was inevitable with the struggles we had when we came to this barren piece of land. Or with the wall that went up around her after her father died. He was a distant and unbending man of old Prussian stock, and whatever was unresolved between them would remain so forever. He, too, could never quite accept the Jew in me.

When we stepped from the ship at Fremantle the day was hot and hard and bright. It reminded me of that first time I set foot on Australian soil, the sea like silver, the air above the iron sheds swimming like water below the dazzling blue. The heat in Adelaide was different: humid and oppressive, a scorching north wind blew. From West Beach airport we could see the hills, clouded by red dust. It should have been a warning.

We were to have three more months of happiness, the three months on the river, with the wasps and the lizards and the moth-gobbling frogs, the soaring pelicans and the snakes basking on the rocks in the sunset. They were the happiest days of our life together, and when we left the river, we left our happiness behind. The five acres of bush that were to have been our paradise became a purgatory that drove us apart, and when it seemed that we would find each other again, the ghost of Ingrid's father stepped between us.

I fled to Cynthia. Cynthia and Ingrid, both Cancers with the Moon conjunct my Mars in Scorpio; friends who know both say they are very much alike. But in Ingrid's horoscope, the influence of Pluto is softened. Cynthia's natal Pluto touches her Sun. Pluto is the planet of extremes. Well-aspected it gives magnetic attraction, strong will and power, but it can also be materialistic, manipulative and cruel.

My ephemeris is open on the table, and my finger traces the position of the planets. Uranus is semisquare Pluto in Scorpio, a time of disintegration. Pluto and Uranus are transiting my Mars: a build-up of aggression that demands a release in violence, the explosion that will shatter what remains of my life.

The horsemen of the Apocalypse, the thunder of the hooves is becoming louder.

When I have murdered Cynthia, my life will be over. Yes, murdered. My killing of Cleaver will be an execution, but Cynthia's death will be murder. I thought that I could kill Cynthia gently and with compassion. I know now that it will be an act of horror, and that afterwards I won't be able to live with its image. But I must kill her, because I love her: not with the abstract, idealised love of self-renunciation – of that I am incapable – but with a sensual, possessive love from which only her death will free me. And then I must end my life.

If my great horse pistol had been more reliable, I would be dead now, my brain blown out of my skull. Fate spared me for a few short days so that I could complete my work.

'I pulled the trigger against myself,' I scream at Cleaver, 'and you have the gall to question my courage.'

'Any fool can commit suicide,' he says with contempt. 'It takes courage to keep on living.'

'Think of Helga,' cries Mupp from the wardrobe. 'Think of your daughter.'

'I want to end the pain, the pain, the pain,' I bellow.

'Coward,' calls Mupp.

'Coward,' calls Cleaver.

Suicide, cowardice or courage? Uncle Oswald leapt from a window at Steinhof. He leapt from a pantry window barely wide enough to squeeze through, a window so narrow that no one had thought it necessary to have it barred. A sign of Uncle

Oswald's determination. And Grandfather Zdenko killed himself for honour, the honour of the Danube monarchy. He died in his blue dress uniform, with white gloves and sash and sword.

Hitler committed suicide in his bunker.

My bunker is this timber and asbestos shack on a barren patch of ground under the hard blue sky.

Once again, the pain flares up inside me; my belly is a furnace. They could have installed my belly in the crematorium at Auschwitz. They could have burned corpses in my belly.

The hooves of the horsemen thunder in my ears.

27

HEAVY CLOUDS are gathering to the north. It is slate-grey dawn. I drop the blind. I have not slept. My face in the bathroom mirror is puffy, my eyes bloodshot, the loose skin of my lower lids stippled from crying, my hair and beard matted. The room tilts like a ship at sea. I grip the basin for support.

'Look at you,' says Mupp. 'Cynthia might be with you now if you hadn't let yourself go. You ought to be ashamed of yourself. You were something once. What happened? How did you come to this?'

'I needed her.' My tears of self-pity return. 'With her at my side, I would have made a fresh start.'

'Don't pass the buck. You can't blame Cynthia for your misery. Only you can pull yourself out of your mess. No one else will.'

I moan.

'Where is your self-respect? Jack has self-respect. Even Cleaver has self-respect. Look at you. A little Jew who loves Hitler.'

'I'm not a little Jew.'

'You're a little Jew because you act like a little Jew. It's very convenient for you to play the victim. "Please, world, I'm only a little Jew, love me, don't send me to the gas chamber." '

My head is splitting. 'Stop it!'

'If you're going to be a Jew, then be a big Jew. You can be anything you want to be. Grow up, that's all.'

A flock of black cockatoos descends from the sky. The air is full of the swish of their wings and the eeea-eeea of their screeching. They settle, hundreds of them, in the trees and bushes. The clouds are massing overhead. It is stifling, oppressive, and I am slippery with sweat. A silver tongue of lightning flickers above the horizon. Seconds later comes the roll of the thunder, then another flash, closer, the thunderclap rattles the windows, and the cockatoos take wing, their startled screeches fading into the distance. The first heavy drops splatter in the dust. I stand naked in the open, my arms and face raised, and feel the sting of the rain on my skin, the water running into my eyes. The thirsty ground drinks greedily. Then the heavens open, the rain pelts down like nails. I flee inside. A solid wall of water blots out the day. The gutters run over, and water washes down the window panes and floods in under the door. The drumming on the iron roof is deafening. The dust turns to mud, the mud slides down the hill. But it still rains, it rains now as if it will rain forever. After the parched months when it seemed that it would never rain again.

I sit in the unnatural darkness, my ears filled with the crash of the rain. My welcome and relief at the first drops have changed to dread, my teeth are on edge. In vain I clamp my hands over my ears. I can't shut out the noise. Water drips from the ceiling, spatters the typewriter and books and papers on the table, and forms pools on the floor. I watch, paralysed. When will the house float down the hill? The leak becomes a stream, and I still can't move; my manuscript is a sodden pile.

Only slowly do I become aware of the silence. The rain has stopped, the temperature has fallen and I shiver. But I am still unable, or unwilling, to move. The water continues to drip from the ceiling on to the table, and from the table to the floor.

The jackpump is no longer clunking and shrieking. It has been switched off, or short-circuited by the rain. The only sounds are the dripping of the water from the ceiling and the tick of the little pendulum clock with the hand-painted face that Ingrid once gave me.

Hitler in the tape deck: 'I will exterminate you!'

I erase the tape.

The water has stopped dripping from the ceiling. Now there is just the ticking of the clock.

From the wardrobe, I fetch Mupp. I straighten out his socks and his pink baby dress and sit him beside the typewriter. I spin a new sheet of paper into the machine. I will begin again, I will write about the river, its magic, the yellow wasp with the black-banded belly that built its nest on the back of the food safe, the blue-tongue lizard, the frogs with their suction-cup toes, the snakes curled up on the rocks in the sunsets and the pelicans soaring past. I tap out:

Chapter One